AN IMPOSSIBLE COINCIDENCE

Is this Evan Murphy? YES. NO. DONE TAGGING.

"What the hell?" I said.

Toni brought her face closer to the screen. "Who's Evan Murphy?"

"I don't know, but FriendShare seems to think he's my dead boyfriend."

She shook her head. "Stupid website. It's probably glitchy or something. Just say 'no' and then hit 'post.'"

My finger hovered over the mouse, but I didn't click "no." My muscles tightened into steel coils. It was probably nothing. It *had* to be nothing. But I needed to see.

With a trembling hand, I clicked on Evan's name.

"What are you doing?" Toni asked.

"I just want to see who he is," I said. "Now I'm curious."

"You're postponing the closure. I knew you'd chicken out. You need to do this!"

She continued to lovingly lecture me, but I couldn't hear her anymore. All I heard was the rush of blood through my head and the ragged, sharp intakes of my own breath.

Because the page had loaded. Evan Murphy lived a few towns away and looked *exactly* like Flynn. Except he was very much alive.

OTHER BOOKS YOU MAY ENJOY

FORGET ME

FORGET ME
FORGET ME
FORGET ME
FORGET ME
FORGET ME
FORGET ME
FORGET ME
FORGET ME
FORGET ME
FORGET ME
FORGET ME

K. A. HARRINGTON

speak

An Imprint of Penguin Group (USA)

SPEAK
Published by the Penguin Group
Penguin Group (USA) LLC
375 Hudson Street
New York, New York 10014

USA * Canada * UK * Ireland * Australia
New Zealand * India * South Africa * China

penguin.com
A Penguin Random House Company

First published in the United States of America by G. P. Putnam's Sons,
an imprint of Penguin Group (USA) LLC, 2014
Published by Speak, an imprint of Penguin Group (USA) LLC, 2015

THE LIBRARY OF CONGRESS HAS CATALOGED THE G. P. PUTNAM'S SONS
EDITION AS FOLLOWS:
Harrington, Kim, date
Forget me / K.M. Harrington. pages cm
Summary: In a town suffering after the major employer closed under a cloud
of scandal, Morgan and her friends uncover a mystery as they try to learn if
her supposedly dead boyfriend is living nearby under a different name.
[1. Mystery and detective stories. 2. Secrets—Fiction. 3. Murder—Fiction.
4. Friendship—Fiction. 5. Dating (Social customs)—Fiction. 6. Family
life—Massachusetts—Fiction. 7. Massachusetts—Fiction.] I. Title.
PZ7.H23817For 2014 [Fic]—dc23 2013026298
ISBN: 978-0-399-16529-0 (hardcover)

Speak ISBN 978-0-14-750941-3

Printed in the United States of America

10 9 8 7 6 5 4 3 2 1

*To Susan, who would punch me
if I wrote anything sappy here.*

FORGET ME

PROLOGUE

PROLOGUE

PROLOGUE

PROLOGUE

PROLOGUE

He lied to me.

That was my first thought when I saw him.

I was alone in my car, on the way to the party where Toni and my other friends were waiting. As I drove down Lincoln Road, my eyes went to the tall chain-link fence that bordered the old amusement park. In the distance, I could almost make out the highest hill of the kiddie coaster and the happy dragon that towered over the bumper cars. But it was dark, so I might have just been seeing what I knew was there.

What I *wasn't* expecting to see was my boyfriend, Flynn. The car's headlights reflected off his pale face, which seemed to almost float in the darkness. Flynn had told me he couldn't come because he had plans with his parents.

I slammed on my brakes, shifted into reverse, and pulled over. Squinting into the darkness, I hoped the light had played a trick on me. But there he was, leaning against the fence.

Caught, he walked swiftly toward the car, head down. His

ratty black trench coat fluttered open in the wind, revealing dark jeans and the vintage U2 T-shirt I'd bought him. He rapped his knuckles on the passenger-side window, and I lowered it.

He rested his arms on the roof of the car and hung his head low to look in the window. "Hey, Morgan."

"What are you doing out here?" I asked, trying to keep my voice cool and level.

"Just hanging out, thinking."

Brooding was Flynn's natural state, but he seemed even more depressed than usual. Maybe he hadn't lied after all. Maybe he really did have plans with his family but they'd had a fight or something. And he came out here to get away.

"Did something happen?" I asked. "You could've called me. I would've picked you up."

"I know . . ." His voice was strained, different. He had a complicated relationship with his parents and hated to talk about them at all. I never forced him to let me in. I figured he would when he was ready. He'd moved to town two months ago, and I was the only one he ever voluntarily talked to. I told myself he just needed more time than most people, that was all.

He straightened to his full height, and I couldn't see his face through the window anymore. I wanted to look him in the eye. I needed to quiet the uncertainty whispering from the back of my mind. I killed the engine and got out of the car.

"What are you doing?" he said.

"Coming to talk to you." I walked through the headlights, rested a hand on the warm hood, and stared at him.

But he wouldn't look at me. His eyes were jittery, nervous. They kept roaming over my shoulder to watch the road, like he was expecting another car.

This end of Lincoln Road was never busy after the amusement park shut down years ago. The only people who used it were those who knew it connected to the back of Meadow Place—the half-empty development of McMansions—where I'd been heading before I saw him. But I was hours late to the party. Everyone was already there. So who was he expecting to come down this deserted road? Was he . . . meeting someone else?

"Flynn . . ." I pushed his name out of my tightened throat. "What are you really doing out here?"

He looked down the street once more, and his expression changed. He seemed to come to some decision. "Get in the car."

I blinked, confused. "What?"

He opened the passenger door quickly, and motioned for me to get in on the other side. I dashed around and slid into the driver's seat. He leaned across the space between us and gave me a quick kiss. Like I'd just picked him up for a date, not found him acting shady by the side of the road.

He reached over and started the engine. "Let's go."

His sudden change had my head spinning. "What's the rush?"

"Let's just get out of here. I want to be with you." He pointed at the road. "Let's go somewhere."

"The party?"

"Anywhere you want."

I pulled onto the road and drove slowly. This behavior wasn't entirely surprising. Flynn was normally secretive and moody, regarding most people and things with a quiet disdain. But that's why he made me feel special. I was the thing he *didn't* hate. I was the person who could make him crack a smile by calling him "Mr. Serious." Just two weeks ago, pressing against a bare-limbed tree on a frosty night, our lips inches apart, he told me I was the only good thing in his life.

But now, he rubbed both hands on his thighs as his left leg bounced up and down. He reminded me of a caged animal, yearning to break out and run free. But no one was making him sit here. I hadn't forced him to get in the car.

I gave him a playful poke in the side. "Look who it is! It's Mr. Serious."

But he didn't smile this time. Instead, he cast a quick glance over his shoulder at the dark road behind us. I didn't speak, hoping the silence would encourage him to tell me what he was thinking. But the more time went on, the more I worried. Images flashed in my mind, of another girl driving this road, looking for Flynn at their predetermined meeting spot. She was prettier than me, maybe older, cooler, edgier. She knew bands

I'd never heard of. Liked art and philosophical discussions. She had a dark side to her, one that Flynn found very attractive.

I forced the thought out of my head. I was driving myself crazy.

Maybe I was being paranoid. Maybe he wasn't expecting someone else. He was just standing out there at night in the dark because that's a weird, loner, *Flynn* thing to do.

He looked in the side-view mirror.

"What's going on, Flynn?" I asked.

A lock of black hair fell across his eyes. "What do you mean?"

"Something's up with you. Why were you standing out there? Why are you acting nervous? Tell me what's going on," I demanded. I never had attitude with him. I always went with the flow, did what he wanted, never questioned his idiosyncrasies. I never wanted to be *that* girlfriend. Nagging. Annoying. But tonight was different. I felt different.

He stared at me. I tried to keep my eyes on the road, but I could still feel him looking at me. What was he thinking? I'd have given anything to know.

"You can pull over and let me out here," he said quietly.

"What?" There was nothing but woods surrounding us. He'd have to walk a mile to get to the nearest house. He'd rather do that than *talk* to me?

"I'm not in the mood to go to one of your friend's lame parties."

Holy mood swing. I raised my eyebrows. "Nice, Flynn. Real nice. My friends have been nothing but good to you even though you seem to feel that you're above them for some reason."

"I'm not above them. I just have no interest in them. I only want to be with you."

"Then be with me," I pleaded. "We can go somewhere and talk."

But he was already shaking his head. "I don't want to talk."

"You have to let me in, Flynn. I can't keep going on like this."

"Then pull over," he snapped.

I turned to look at him. His eyes were apprehensive, but his voice was so sure, so filled with venom. He reached for the door handle like he was willing to jump out at thirty miles per hour. The tires squealed as I slammed on the brakes and the car jumped up onto the curb.

"Why are you doing this?" I yelled. "Why are you acting like this?"

His mouth opened and his eyes flicked around, like they were searching for the answer in the air. "Because I don't want this," he said finally. "You, driving around town, checking up on me, making sure I'm where I told you I was."

"I wasn't doing that," I said indignantly. "I was on my way to the party. It's not my fault you happened to be on the side of the road I was driving on. Excuse me for pulling over to say hi to my boyfriend who was standing alone in the dark like a creep."

"I have the right to stand wherever and however I want."

"I never said you didn't!"

He shook his head. "It's just . . . I think . . . it's time for us to be over."

His words took a moment to sink in. I'd thought we were having our first fight. Apparently it was also our last. "You're . . . breaking up with me?"

I saw him swallow. Then he nodded, once.

I squared my shoulders. I would not cry. I would not give him one ounce of emotion. "Why?"

He opened his mouth to answer, but then closed it again.

"I have to go," he said softly. He pushed open the door and shoved it closed behind him. His coat flapped in the breeze as he walked down the road, into the dark night.

My hands tightened on the steering wheel and tears spilled from my eyes, clouding my vision as I watched him walk away, until he was just a wavy, indistinct form far down the dark road.

I didn't hear the car, but I saw the headlights come around the bend. Too fast.

My back bolted straight, and my lungs froze. For one long moment, I couldn't breathe in or release what was held in my chest. I could only watch as Flynn flew through the air, flipping like a tossed doll. Then he crashed back down, his body rolling and scraping across the asphalt.

The SUV kept going.

It barreled past me, a black bullet with tinted windows, too fast for me to catch a look at the plate.

I have no memory of getting out of the car or running to Flynn with the cold air lashing my tearstained cheeks. I only remember holding his head in my lap. Seeing his blood on the ground. Listening to the 911 operator on my cell telling me to stay calm.

When the ambulance came, my hand was on Flynn's chest.

His heart was still beating.

CHAPTER 1
CHAPTER 1
CHAPTER 1
CHAPTER 1
CHAPTER 1

I lifted the camera to my eye and focused on the lion's mouth. *Click.* Born of metal, plastic, and paint, he'd been a happy lion, with rounded teeth and lips curving into a smile. But now the paint was chipped, the plastic cracked, and bits of exposed metal were rusted. Graffiti morphed his happy smile into a sharp-toothed, menacing grin. Larry the Lion once welcomed children to King's Fantasy World Amusement Park. Now he warned people to stay away.

Inside the park there were many more shots waiting to be taken. The fun house with its broken windows. The thick weeds that climbed the track of the kiddie coaster. The mice that nested in the Skee-Ball holes. But I didn't climb the fence to enter the park.

Not that the No Trespassing sign intimidated me. Those were posted all over town, and they never stopped anyone. A rule meant nothing if there was no consequence for breaking it. No one was monitoring these places. Maybe at first, five years ago, when everything shut down, officers would swing by in a patrol car. But now . . . no one cared anymore.

The reason I wasn't going past the fence was that the last time I was inside King's Fantasy World, I met Flynn. My boyfriend. Who was now dead.

He'd been gone three months, and I still wasn't ready to revisit those memories.

I wasn't ready to say good-bye.

My town, River's End, had once been a shimmering oasis in our drab, rural area of central Massachusetts. But after the town's only major employer, Stell Pharmaceuticals, went under, several other businesses that relied on Stell soon followed, and River's End began its steep and sudden decline. Now half the McMansions stood empty. The mall's doors were shuttered. Happy Time Mini Golf was overgrown. And, saddest of all the forgotten places, King's Fantasy World was abandoned and rotting.

What used to be the happiest place in town was now the scariest.

I checked the display on my camera. The focus of that last shot could've been better. I adjusted and tried again. *Click*. Using my hand to shade the viewing screen from the sun, I squinted and then smiled. This one was a keeper. It captured what I was going for. The lion wasn't evil. He was just . . . lonely.

I packed my camera back into its bag and drove home. It

was enough that I'd finally gotten that shot of Larry the Lion. I'd save climbing the fence for some other day.

I pulled my car into our empty driveway, not surprised that my parents were out. They used Saturdays to catch up on all the things they couldn't do during the work week: grocery shopping, the post office, the bank, the pharmacy. A never-ending list of errands.

My parents had both been biochemists for Stell. Great jobs, great money. But then people started dying from Stell's most popular product, a migraine pill. The company shut down and everyone lost their jobs. Even people who didn't directly work for Stell but depended on Stell employees to spend their money in town—at restaurants, retail stores—were out of work. Some businesses hung on longer than others, but eventually most had to give up and close their doors.

Now Dad took the train into Boston for work, a two-hour commute each way. Mom worked here in town but needed two jobs to earn anywhere near what she used to make at her previous job. But at least they *had* work. Not everyone in town was so lucky.

I swung the camera bag over my shoulder and closed the car door with my hip. I smirked as I spied Toni sitting on the front steps. Toni Klane was my best friend and had been since we were little. Her house was one street over, but lately it seemed like she lived with me.

She visibly shivered as she stood up. It was the end of March. That week that always seemed like such a tease. It was still cold, but spring was so close, you could almost smell it in the air. Toni wore jeans and a scoop-neck T-shirt, her arms wrapped around her abdomen. I'm sure she didn't mean to forget a sweatshirt or a coat. Sometimes she just had to leave her house in a hurry.

"Morgan Tulley, where have you been?" she said, tapping her foot in mock impatience. "Out snapping photos of creepy things?"

"Nope. Flowers," I deadpanned.

Her face brightened momentarily and then shut back down. "You're joking."

"Of course I am."

She smacked my arm.

I unlocked the front door and we hurried inside, the warm air a welcome greeting. I didn't have to ask why she'd come over without texting or calling first. Why she was sitting on my front steps for who knew how long, shivering in the cold, waiting for me. If she wanted to talk about the Fight of the Day, she would. Most days, she'd rather not.

Toni's parents were having more trouble than most. The unemployment money was about to run dry, but the liquor was overflowing. Her family was exploding, and if Toni hung around the house all day, she'd be sliced by shrapnel. Collateral damage. So when she showed up here, I never turned her away.

I grabbed some sodas and a bag of Doritos from the kitchen. I wasn't hungry, but I knew Toni probably was, and she'd never help herself no matter how many times I told her it was okay. We climbed the stairs to the second floor and went into my room: our sanctuary. It had all-white furniture and bright, lime-green walls. I used to think it looked like the happiest room in the world, but now it felt like it was just pretending to be happy. If a room could feign emotion.

While Toni flopped onto the bed and opened the chips, I sat at my desk and uploaded the photos I'd taken to my laptop.

"Larry the Lion, huh?" Toni said between crunches.

"Yeah. I finally got that shot I've been trying for."

"The one that makes him look lonely and not like a jacked-up plastic lion that wants to eat your face?"

"Exactly." Even though my back was to her, I smiled. It was nice to know someone listened to me when I babbled about my photography.

"Are you going to submit it now?" she asked through a mouthful of chips.

I'd been building my portfolio to apply for a summer course at the local college. It was a small class and highly selective. "Nah. It's not ready."

"You won't ever think it's ready," Toni huffed. "Then you won't have to apply and risk being rejected."

Toni's favorite hobby was psychoanalyzing me. I cast a look at her over my shoulder. "I'll apply. Just not yet."

She pointed a chip at me. "No offense, Morgan, but you've always been the kind of girl who sits back and lets things happen to her."

I resisted an eye roll. "And who should I be?"

"The kind of girl who goes out and *makes* things happen."

I saved the photos and shut my laptop. "Believe me. I want to be in this program. That's why I'm taking my time. My portfolio has to be perfect." I was a little aggravated, but knew her nagging came from a good place. I playfully stuck my tongue out. "So stop pressuring me."

She made a face right back. "I'm your best friend, that's my job." She paused, and her casual tone turned serious. "So did you go . . . *into* the park?"

I shook my head. "Not today."

"How are you doing . . . *today*?" She emphasized the last word.

I should've known she'd remember the date. Three months ago today Flynn was killed in a hit-and-run accident. I hadn't gotten any messages or calls from my other friends. My parents never mentioned Flynn much after his death. They were raised in the school of "the problem doesn't exist if you don't talk about it."

But Toni remembered. She knew today would be hard on me. That's what I loved about her. Her world was chaos back home, but she still worried about me.

I opened my laptop again and pretended to be doing something important. "I'm all right."

"Look at me," she demanded.

I twisted around to face her.

"He's been gone now longer than you were together," she said, meeting my eyes.

Technically, she was right. We'd only dated for about two months, and he'd been dead for three, but that didn't make it okay. It wasn't like there was some grief formula. If you knew someone for X amount of time and he'd been dead for Y amount of time, you will be over the whole thing in X plus Y divided by Z.

I wish it were that simple.

"I just hate to see you so sad," she said.

"Lots of people in the world are sad," I countered.

"But they're not my best friend. Who cares about those losers?" She cracked a smile, and I mirrored it.

"I get what you're saying," I said and gave a little shrug. "But I can't just magically shut the feelings off, you know?"

She sat up straighter on the bed and folded her legs underneath her. "What if we nudged it along?"

I narrowed my eyes. "What do you mean?"

"It's the three-month anniversary of Flynn's death. Maybe you should do something closure-y."

"I love the way you make up words by putting a *y* at the end of them."

"I love the way you avoid a conversation you don't want to have by making an astute observation about me."

"Don't you mean astute-y?"

"Morgan."

"Okay, okay. What would you like me to do?"

"Just some kind of closure."

I leaned back in the chair and racked my brain. "Like . . . toss a wreath into the river to symbolize how he's drifted away from me?"

Toni rolled her eyes. "Nothing that cheesy. We can start with something simple like . . ." She chewed on the ends of her sandy-blond hair for a moment. "Upload a pic of him to FriendShare with a good-bye message or something."

"How is that any form of closure?" I asked.

"It's public. It's showing your friends—who are worried about you, by the way—that you're starting to heal and move on. Having the balls to say something publicly makes it mean more."

"I don't have balls. I have girly parts."

She threw a Dorito at me, but it wasn't very aerodynamic and landed on the floor halfway between us. "Take this seriously, please."

"Flynn hated FriendShare," I pointed out.

"No offense, hon, but that boy hated everything except you."

I shrugged. "He was just private. People have the right to be private."

Toni placed a finger in her open mouth and pretended to gag. "He refused to talk about himself. He never invited you to his house."

"He had family issues," I said.

"He had issues, all right."

I didn't want to get into this. I had always known Toni didn't like Flynn. And he hadn't exactly made an effort to be likable to her, either. I'd found his private nature mysterious and sexy. She'd found it "douchey." But she never told me to break up with him and hardly ever complained. If the roles had been reversed and she'd been dating a boy I hated, I would've nagged her a lot more.

I searched her dark eyes. This small act of closure seemed important to her. And what did I have to lose? Maybe it would make me feel a little better.

"Fine," I said, giving in. "I'll do it."

She clapped and beamed like the proud parent of a child who'd made the right choice.

I logged in to FriendShare. My profile picture came up, a photo of Toni and me taken last year. We had our arms around each other's shoulders, which was a little awkward since I was so much taller than her. I glanced in the mirror resting on my desk and then back at the picture. It's amazing how a photo can tell you so much about a person in one quick glance. In the picture, my blue eyes were brighter, my black hair shinier. I glowed. Everything about me in the mirror now seemed dulled in comparison.

This was the right thing to do. I had to get on the "path of healing" (to quote one of Toni's well-meaning speeches).

I paused with my hands over the keys, then typed: *Gone, but not forgotten.*

"Good," Toni said from over my shoulder. "That's good."

Then I clicked to upload the only picture I had of Flynn. One that he hadn't even known I'd taken. I took it the first day I met him, in King's Fantasy World. I went into the park to get shots for my portfolio and stumbled upon this mysterious boy, all alone, and it was like my camera had a mind of its own.

The icon in the center of the application swirled for a moment as the photo loaded. Then Flynn's face filled the screen. My chest squeezed as I fought off the urge to cry. Even in this innocuous photo, he seemed like a tragic figure. Leaning against the wall of the fun house, full lips slightly parted, his face tilted just a degree as his steely gray eyes searched for the source of the sound in the abandoned park. The sound had been me.

The outline of a box opened around his head as Friend-Share's facial recognition software attempted to tag him with a name. It was a handy application if you were uploading a big group picture or a bunch of photos that you wanted done quickly. But I knew it was a waste of time for this picture. Flynn had never been on FriendShare. He thought it was "weird" and "intrusive." Which was an observation I found poignant and smart, and Toni again found douchey.

But the operation ended and a message read:

Is this Evan Murphy? YES. NO. DONE TAGGING.

"What the hell?" I said.

Toni brought her face closer to the screen. "Who's Evan Murphy?"

"I don't know, but FriendShare seems to think he's my dead boyfriend."

She shook her head. "Stupid website. It's probably glitchy or something. Just say 'no' and then hit 'post.'"

My finger hovered over the mouse, but I didn't click "no." My muscles tightened into steel coils. It was probably nothing. It *had* to be nothing. But I needed to see.

With a trembling hand, I clicked on Evan's name.

"What are you doing?" Toni asked.

"I just want to see who he is," I said. "Now I'm curious."

"You're postponing the closure. I knew you'd chicken out. You need to do this!"

She continued to lovingly lecture me, but I couldn't hear her anymore. All I heard was the rush of blood through my head and the ragged, sharp intakes of my own breath.

Because the page had loaded. Evan Murphy lived a few towns away and looked *exactly* like Flynn. Except he was very much alive.

CHAPTER 2
CHAPTER 2
CHAPTER 2
CHAPTER 2

CHAPTER 2

Doritos hit the floor as the open bag fell from Toni's hand. "Whoa . . ."

"Yeah," I breathed.

"What? Who?"

Toni continued her one-word questions as I clicked around, trying to access anything else on Evan Murphy's page. But he had a good amount of privacy settings on, and the only thing I could see was that one small profile picture and his town name, Littlefield—only fifteen minutes away.

Toni jabbed a finger at the photo. "It's Flynn. I mean, it *is* him, right?"

"It can't be," I said. "I don't know."

"How can you not know?" Toni screeched. "FriendShare matched his face to this guy. It's him! Look!"

I didn't know how I was staying so calm. Toni was clearly going bananas. But it was like my brain had shut off all emotion so it could focus. I clicked on the photo in an attempt to enlarge it, but the resolution was terrible when I tried to zoom in. The face was Flynn's face. Those steely gray eyes that were so hard to ignore. The slope of his jaw. The sly, one-sided grin.

But it couldn't be him. I searched for something sane to grasp on to.

"He's wearing a baseball hat," I said quickly. "Flynn never wore hats."

"He also never said his name was Evan Murphy and he lived in Littlefield. Being an undercover hat lover obviously wasn't his biggest secret."

I needed to get away from the computer, from the familiar face smiling at me on the screen. I pushed the chair back and stood up. "It's just someone who looks eerily like him."

"Not eerily," Toni said. "Exactly."

I pulled my hair back and held it at the nape of my neck. "Could he, like, have a twin living in another town with a different last name?" I said, thinking out loud. "I know it's crazy, but what else could it be?"

"He could be alive," Toni said.

I sank down onto the edge of my bed as a wave of nausea washed over me. I put my face in my hands and rubbed circles on my forehead. Could Flynn really be alive? How would that be possible? And . . . he let me think he was dead? Would he do that? *How* could he do that?

I dropped my hands and looked up at Toni. She was staring at me with a wary expression, probably waiting for me to lose it.

"It's impossible," I said.

"There was no funeral," she countered.

That was true. I'd never met Flynn's parents. He never wanted to talk about them, and I assumed he never told them about me. I never got word about a wake or funeral, and it wasn't printed in the paper. Flynn had lived in town only a couple of months, and he didn't even go to our school. He went to St. Pelagius. He didn't know anyone in town. I always assumed his family had a memorial service back where they'd come from. Somewhere in New Hampshire.

But now my brain was going haywire. No one I knew had seen his body. So how did I really know he was dead?

"The last time you saw him," Toni said gently, "he was still alive, right?"

"Yeah, but a nurse at the hospital told me he didn't make it."

Toni shrugged. "Maybe she was wrong. The hospital has a gazillion patients. She could've mixed things up, thought you were asking about someone else."

I paused. That night was such a blur, especially in the hospital. I hadn't been allowed past the waiting area. I called my parents. I was hysterical, to the point where a doctor prescribed a sedative, which my mom gave me when they forced me to go home. It wasn't until the next morning, when I woke and called the hospital, that I found out Flynn was dead.

"But the cops came and took a statement," I said. As useless as it had been. All I'd seen was a black SUV. I hadn't seen the plate. I couldn't even accurately pick out the make or model from the book they'd shown me.

"Did the cops say he was dead?" Toni asked.

I searched my fuzzy memory. "I don't think so. I just remember them asking me to describe the vehicle."

Toni sat beside me on the bed and ran her hand over the goose bumps on my forearm. "A hit-and-run doesn't have to end in death to be a crime," she said. "The police would still come investigate."

I shook my head until my neck felt sore. This was crazy. Crazier than crazy. To even entertain the slight possibility that Flynn could be alive . . . it was nuts.

"Just think it through," Toni said anxiously. "What evidence do you have of his death? He was alive when they put him in the ambulance. The only person who ever told you he was dead was a nurse, who could've been talking about the wrong patient."

What if he didn't die? And then he, what? Just . . . slipped away? Became someone else?

No. I wasn't going to be lured by Toni's crazy-talk. She was notorious for jumping to the wildest conclusions. A neighbor talked too long to the mailman—affair! Birds fell from the sky in Guatemala—aliens! I usually rolled my eyes and ignored her insanity. But I had to admit, this time, as ridiculous as it sounded, it held a kernel of possibility.

Or maybe I just wanted it to be true.

Toni walked over to my desk and put her hand on the mouse.

"What are you doing?" I asked.

"Sending him a friend request."

In one swift motion, I rose and pulled her hand away. "No, don't."

"Why not?"

"If he's not Flynn, what would we even say? 'Hey, don't mind us, you just look exactly like this dead kid.'"

Toni's eyes traveled back to the photo. "And if it *is* Flynn?"

"Then I don't want to scare him away. I don't want him to know I found him. Not yet."

CHAPTER 3
CHAPTER 3
CHAPTER 3
CHAPTER 3

CHAPTER 3

The next morning I got ready for school on autopilot. I showered, dressed, and headed downstairs for breakfast. I passed the long mahogany table in the dining room that we only used on holidays when my grandparents came to visit from Florida. Day to day we ate casually, at a small round table in the nook of the kitchen, perfect for three. Or two. Or sometimes, just me.

I ate a bowl of cereal, the clinking of the spoon echoing in the quiet, my mind drifting. I snapped out of my trance when Mom bounded into the kitchen.

"I'm heading to work," she said, kissing my cheek as I rinsed my bowl in the sink. A line of gray shimmered from the part in her hair, a reminder of the extra time and money she no longer had available to spend at the salon. "I made you lunch. It's in the fridge."

"You didn't have to make me lunch, Mom." She got up at some ungodly hour every morning to get things done—laundry, bill paying, ironing Dad's shirts before he left for work, etc. Juggling two jobs, she had to find the time where she could. "I can do it myself. I know you're rushing."

She gave me a little smile, but it barely disguised her exhaustion. That's how my family operated. Always polite and pleasant, never acknowledging the real feelings beneath the perma-smiles. Even I played along. Whenever college came up, I always told my parents I was only a junior and I'd worry about it next year. But the truth was, I worried about it now. A lot. Thoughts of choices and applications and financial aid sometimes kept me up at night. But I didn't want to add more to their stack of Things to Worry About. For all I knew, that could be the thing to finally bring the pile crashing down. I preferred our tradition of pleasant denial.

Mom reached out and tucked a strand of hair behind my ear. "I'm working double shifts today, so I won't be home for dinner. And Dad . . . well, you know his hours. So making your lunch was the least I could do."

She picked at a fingernail and forced a smile, but I knew she felt guilty. She hated that I was here alone so much.

"Don't worry about dinner," I said, grabbing the paper sack from the fridge. "Toni and I have plans anyway."

Lies flowed easily from me when I thought they'd make people feel better. Maybe I'd ask Toni to go out for pizza to turn it into a truth.

"Great," Mom said cheerily. "You girls have fun!"

I kept the perma-smile on until she walked out the door.

River's End High School was built when the town was thriving. As things went downhill and people moved away, our schools thinned out. Teachers were laid off. Classrooms were closed and locked, their heating vents shut off to save money. Sometimes I found myself drawn to these unused rooms, with their empty desks and blank boards, feeling the draft of cold air seeping out from under the crack of the door.

This morning I went right to my locker. I was there for only thirty seconds before Toni appeared, from out of nowhere. She had this way of moving silently, like a ninja.

She leaned into me and whispered, "How are you doing . . . ?"

I took a deep breath. "It's all I can think about, but I don't know what to do. The first step would be figuring out if Evan is a real person. It could be a fake profile page or something. If only I had a mutual friend in common, I could try to find out more, but I don't."

Toni smiled. "I do."

"What?"

"Last night, I logged in to my account at home and brought up Evan's page. We have one mutual friend."

I closed my locker and held my books to my chest. "Who?"

She grimaced like she'd just taken a bite of something bitter. "Reece Childs."

Ugh. I rolled my eyes. "Too Cool Reece?"

"He's worth talking to for five minutes if we can find out who Evan is."

Reece was the party king and walked the halls with an over-confident swagger, flirting with girls and calling out to his "bros." He was one of the fakest people in our grade. A douche of the highest order. Toni and I had nicknamed him "Too Cool Reece." Online he friended anyone he'd ever met and even some people he hadn't. He sent me a friend request once, and I ignored it. I was picky about who I approved. Meanwhile, Reece had thousands on his list.

But apparently one of them was Evan Murphy.

I drew my lips tight, determined. "Fine. When are we doing this?"

Toni motioned over my shoulder. "How about now?"

I turned around and, sure enough, there was Too Cool Reece taking a gulp of water from the fountain. He dried his mouth with the back of his hand and started to walk away.

"Hey, Reece, wait up," I called.

He looked at us over the top of his Aviator sunglasses. Seriously. It was cloudy out, not summer, *and* he was inside. "What's up, ladies?" He stretched out the last syllable like it contained ten *z*s.

"Do you know Evan Murphy?" I asked, getting right to the point.

He scrunched his face up as he thought. "Sounds familiar . . ."

"You're friends with him on FriendShare," I added.

He wagged his eyebrows. "You hunting for a new boyfriend, Morgan?"

Toni had been fiddling with her phone and now she held it up. "This guy. You know him?"

Reece bent down to make up for the height difference. "I can't really—"

Toni let out an aggravated sigh. "Take the glasses off, cool guy. Come on."

He pulled his sunglasses off and hung them on the collar of his tight V-neck. He took Toni's phone and stared at Evan's profile photo. "Oh yeah. We played in the same summer baseball league a couple years back. Cool guy. Power hitter. Lives in Littlefield."

Flynn had an athletic frame but never mentioned any interest in sports. That didn't necessarily mean anything, though.

Reece started typing something into Toni's phone.

"Um, what are you doing?" she asked.

"Just giving you my digits."

Toni grabbed the phone out of his hands.

"So the guy's name is really Evan?" I asked.

Reece gave me a strange look. "What else would it be?"

Toni and I exchanged a glance. "Did you ever meet Flynn, my boyfriend?" I asked.

"Nah. I heard about the car thing, though. Sorry."

Not exactly the most delicate way to say it, but the thought was there. "Um, yeah. Thanks."

"Is that all?" Reece said, staring at Toni like he hoped we weren't done with him.

"Yeah," I muttered.

He looked Toni up and down. "If you ever want to hang out . . ." He made the "call me" sign with a hand up to his ear, then turned around and joined the masses.

"Gross." Toni crossed her arms. "What a toolbag."

I let out a long breath. "Well, now we know that Evan exists. He's a real person and has been for at least two years. And he lives in Littlefield just like his profile says."

"But that still doesn't rule out the chance that Flynn *is* him," Toni said.

I slid my books into the crook of my arm. "How so?"

"You never went to Flynn's house. Flynn didn't go to our school. How do you know Flynn wasn't Evan the whole time? Playing some game, telling you lies."

My heart sank at the thought. "Why would a guy do that? To anonymously hook up? Believe me, he didn't get far."

"Maybe he wasn't happy with his life in Littlefield. Maybe he just wanted to feel like someone else for a while. Even if it was only a few hours a week." The way she said it made it sound like something she'd consider.

I took a moment to play with the idea, think about how it could've happened. The day we met, Flynn was alone in King's Fantasy World. I went there to take some pictures and found him hanging out around the fun house. He didn't know me, I didn't know him, so maybe he thought it would be fun to try out a new name, a new identity. We hit it off. We met again and again, and the lies built up. Until the night that he decided he didn't want to be Flynn Parkman anymore. Maybe living a double life was fun at first, but then it got tiring.

Maybe *that's* why he wanted to break up with me.

And then a car hit him. But he survived. His parents brought him home from the hospital, and all he had to do to make Flynn go away was to never step foot in River's End again. Never see me again. And, just like that, Flynn would no longer exist. Problem solved.

When I thought about it that way, it was pretty easy.

I started to feel dizzy and was dimly aware of the fact that my breathing sounded like a marathon runner's. I leaned against the wall for support. The conversations passing us in the hall blurred together.

Toni took my books from me. "Are you okay? Do you want to go to the nurse?"

"No," I said, though my voice sounded far away. "I'm fine."

There was a small possibility that Flynn was alive. Out there. Living another life. With a jolt, my ears cleared, and the tunnel vision relaxed. The fog in my brain was replaced with a burning need for answers.

I would not be satisfied until I knew the truth.

Toni's eyes were lined with concern. "What do you want to do?"

I pushed myself off the wall and took my books back from her. "I want to find out if my ex-boyfriend was a liar."

CHAPTER 4
CHAPTER 4
CHAPTER 4
CHAPTER 4
CHAPTER 4

CHAPTER 4

After school, Toni and I got into my little Civic, tossing our bags into the backseat. The engine turned over with a cough, and I joined the line of cars exiting the parking lot.

"So what's the plan?" Toni asked.

We hadn't discussed it in lunch or during classes because I didn't want to talk about the whole Evan/Flynn thing with anyone else. I had other friends, but they were surface friends. I wasn't as close to any of them as I was to Toni. And maybe Flynn had rubbed off on me, but I was feeling private lately.

"I guess we'll just go to my house and try to dig up more online," I said. I slowed the car to a stop at the red light. "I'll just . . . start Googling and figure something out."

"Take a right here," Toni said, pointing toward the center of town.

"Why?" I asked.

"We'll stop by Town Hall. Cooper will know what to do."

Cooper was Toni's older brother. He was a senior at our school, super smart and cute. Though—much to the dismay of every girl in town—very taken. Diana, his longtime girl-friend, was a year older and a freshman at Harvard. He would be joining her in the fall if his financial aid came through. After college they'd get married and have beautiful, valedictorian, Harvard-bound babies.

But Toni was right. If anyone knew how to research, it was Cooper. He could write a term paper in his sleep.

When we were little, Toni and Cooper used to hate each other. It seemed like their main mission in life was to get the other in trouble, and they fought about every single thing, down to who should hold the remote control. It made me glad I was an only child. But since Stell went out of business, their parents lost their jobs, and everything went to hell, there had been a sort of cease-fire. They never actually talked about it, but I'm guessing once the family began to have *real* problems, Toni and Cooper started to rely on each other more and fight less.

I parked in front of the redbrick building. We climbed the concrete stairs and opened the heavy door. The Town Hall was one of the oldest buildings in River's End, and it felt like it—drafty walls, tall ceilings, elaborate wood moldings. I'd never visited Cooper at work, but Toni obviously had. She marched down the main hallway like she belonged there.

"Got a sec?" she called into the second room on the right.

I looked in. Cooper was hunched over a copier that was making grinding noises as papers flew out of the end.

"Yeah, meet me out back by the benches. I'm due for a break." He didn't even look up, just knew his sister's voice.

I followed Toni out the back door and into a miniature courtyard. A few park benches circled a dried-up fountain. I shivered as the cold from the aluminum seat seeped through my jeans.

A couple of minutes later the door opened and Cooper sauntered out, carrying a Styrofoam coffee cup. He had Toni's sandy-blond hair, but was a full foot taller than her. His eyebrows rose at the sight of me. He hadn't realized I was with her.

"Sorry. I should've brought out drinks for you guys, too." He sat between us and tipped the cup in an offer to share.

I shook my head no.

Toni grimaced. "You smell like a metal fish."

"It's that old copy machine. It's nasty, and the room has no ventilation."

"Oh, poor baby," Toni teased.

"Plus Mrs. Willis came in today ranting and raving again."

"Man." Toni shook her head.

"Who's Mrs. Willis?" I asked.

Toni stopped laughing and explained. "Mrs. Willis used to have Cooper's job. She was a full-timer and had worked here for, like, thirty years. They laid her off, changed the job title, and made it part-time. Then they hired a high school kid for minimum wage."

"I jumped at the chance," Cooper said. "You know how many

of my friends can't even find a part-time job? It's only copying, filing, answering phones. Easy stuff. But I had no idea what they'd done to this lady, and now she comes in and yells at me that I *stole* her job. Like I'm personally responsible."

I held back a smile, picturing some little old lady pointing her finger up at Cooper's face. "It's better than mowing lawns," I said, which was Cooper's previous gig.

He gave me a little elbow jab. "Easy for you to say. You have a cool job."

"You wouldn't be saying that if you knew how much they paid me." The local paper had cut their staff photographers a while back and hired freelancers now. I took photos at sports games and school events, and sometimes crime scenes—like when someone toppled some headstones in the cemetery. I submitted photos to my editor. For any shot they used, I got ten bucks. Terrible money, but at least I was doing something I liked. And I didn't have a Mrs. Willis yelling at me.

"So what are you two bums doing following me to work?" Cooper asked. Toni jutted her chin toward me, and he followed with his eyes. "Morgan?"

I suddenly felt tongue-tied. "Um . . . you remember my boyfriend, Flynn Parkman?"

"Yeah, of course. I met him once when you guys came to pick up Toni. Before he . . . before . . . that night," he said with a familiar look of pity.

"I want to find out more about him. I never got to speak to his parents after he died. I just wanted to get more details, I guess." I knew I was barely making sense.

Toni piped up, "She thinks he may have lied about something."

Cooper turned serious. "Why would that matter now?"

Toni looked at me. She had no problem keeping secrets from her brother. They weren't the kind of siblings who told each other everything, so I didn't feel guilty involving her in my lie.

"Just closure, I guess," I said flatly. "Will you help?"

I knew he'd say yes, but he left me hanging for a moment. The corner of his mouth lifted up. "What do I get in return?"

"Free pizza," I said.

"Deal. Pick me up at five."

Sal brought the large pie to our booth and wordlessly dropped it on the end of the table. I used the tips of my fingers to push the silver plate more toward the center, but it was scorching.

"Ouch, ouch, ouch," I muttered.

"It's not really the food I come for," Cooper said from across the table. "It's the customer service."

Sal's wasn't what you'd call fantastic, but it was the only pizza place left in town. Sal and his daughter Ronnie—who looked like a thirty-year-old version of Sal with long hair—ran the place. They worked every day, every position. They made the pizzas, served the pizzas, answered the phones, rang the register.

The floors were black-and-white checkerboard, and the dark brown paneling had been on the walls for so long, they probably permanently smelled of pizza. No matter how much River's End disintegrated, Sal's stayed the same. I had the feeling that everyone could move away and Sal would stay, still making his pizzas. At least we always had that one constant.

I slid a slice onto my paper plate and patted it with a handful of napkins. Within seconds the napkins were soaked in grease.

Next to me in the booth, Toni had dumped a truckload of red hot pepper flakes on her slice, folded it in half, and taken a huge bite.

"Dainty," Cooper said.

"Shut it," she replied through a mouthful.

I wasn't hungry. I just wanted to know what Cooper had found out with the information I'd given him on Flynn.

"So . . . ," I began.

He dropped his slice and rubbed his hands on a napkin. "So I found out a lot and . . . not so much."

I made a "go on" motion with my hand.

"First off," he said, "Flynn didn't go to St. Pelagius."

I'd already felt this in my gut, but hearing it confirmed was like a lance to the heart. Lie number one. How many more would there be?

"I called a friend of a friend who's a senior there. No one by that name went to the school. So maybe he went somewhere else or was homeschooled? Or maybe he'd already graduated? He looked like he could have been about eighteen."

I took a moment to absorb that info. Flynn had told me he was a senior. And I saw him plenty of times with a beat-up-looking notebook. But any time I asked how school was, he'd just answer with some noncommittal "the usual" or "sucks." No elaborate lies about classes and tests, but still. It stung just the same. Why not just tell me the truth? Whatever that was.

After chewing another bite, Cooper said, "It gets even more interesting from there. He told you he lived on Elm, right?"

Flynn had referred to home as "one of those little houses on Elm." At first I thought he'd been embarrassed to have me over because my house was bigger and nicer. But then, after some pushing, he'd told me he had family issues and didn't want me to become a part of it. From the expectant look on Cooper's face, there was more to it than that.

I nodded. "That's what he said, yeah."

"Well, he didn't live on Elm. Actually, I couldn't find a record of his family living *anywhere* in River's End. There's no public listing for that last name in town. I even checked the private listings and voter registrations. No Parkmans."

My breath hitched. I didn't know whether I should feel curious, sad, betrayed, angry. I settled on nauseated. I pushed my plate of grease to the side. Thinking out loud, I asked, "Then where did they live?"

Cooper shrugged. "Maybe they were squatters."

"Eww," Toni said. "That sounds gross."

Cooper ignored her. "Squatters are people who occupy abandoned buildings or houses. They basically live in them for free, without permission, until they're caught. With the number of foreclosed homes in town, we've had a squatter problem the last few years. The police do their best, but they can't catch them all. Especially if they're quiet and don't draw attention to themselves."

An emptiness gnawed at me from deep inside. Flynn had been my boyfriend. He'd kissed my lips, held my hand, listened to me spill my feelings. But he was a walking lie. I didn't know where he'd lived, where he'd gone to school, nothing.

Even if he was dead, it was like he'd been a ghost from day one.

Toni was staring at me, and I could practically read her mind. This development certainly fanned the flames of her theory. Evan was a dead ringer for Flynn. And if Flynn had lied about where he lived and where he went to school . . . what else had he lied about?

"Do you have to head right home?" Toni asked, zipping up her hoodie. The sun was setting, and a bitter wind had taken its place. Dinner ended quickly. I'd lost my appetite after finding out that my dead(?) ex-boyfriend had been promoted from possible creep to pants-on-fire liar. Cooper opted to walk the couple of blocks back to his car at the Town Hall, but Toni stayed with me.

Even though she usually only avoided her house when Cooper was out, she clearly wasn't ready to go home. I mentally calculated the homework I had waiting for me.

"I can stay out a bit longer," I said. "Where do you want to go?"

She flashed a wicked smile. "It's a surprise. Can I drive?"

I tossed her the keys. "As long as you don't crash or dust up my new paint job."

Toni laughed. My car was twelve years old, and the only new thing on it was the rust that had started to grow along the wheel wells. I got in the passenger side as Toni pulled my driver's-side seat forward a couple of inches.

"Great," I joked. "Now my adjustments are all off."

"It's not my fault I'm height impaired. Just for that, I'm moving your mirrors, too."

She pulled into traffic and I turned my gaze to the window. My breath fogged the glass as I watched our town glide by. Not many outsiders wanted to move into River's End, and I understood why. The rotting, empty buildings definitely gave off a sad vibe. But I'd spent my whole life here. The town had seeped into my bones and become part of who I was.

Every intersection held a memory. The bowling alley where I'd had a few birthday parties was now boarded up, a faded Commercial Property For Sale sign tacked to the wood. Happy Time Mini Golf was overgrown, the paint on the small clubhouse peeling. I couldn't even count how many summer afternoons I'd spent there, holding my club tightly, hoping for a hole-in-one, my hands sticky from a fast-melting ice-cream cone.

Before I knew it, I'd reminisced myself out of town, through the next town, and then found myself glancing at an unfamiliar open field as we passed.

"Where are we going?" I asked, coming out of my trance.

Toni kept her voice light. "Littlefield."

I snapped my head toward her. "What?"

"I just want to do a drive-by of Evan Murphy's house. See where he lives. No pressure to knock or anything."

My heart skipped a beat. "How did you get his address?"

"You think my brother's the only one with skills?" She gasped in mock indignation.

"He was publicly listed?" I guessed.

She grinned. "Yeah."

"Thanks." Okay, granted, all she did was type *Murphy* and *Littlefield, MA,* into her phone. But she did it for me. She took charge and drove because she knew I needed answers.

"Don't thank me yet. Let's see what we find out."

The prospect of coming face-to-face with Evan and/or Flynn turned me into a giant rubber-band ball of stress. I'm not a spontaneous person. I like to think things through, plan every angle. Toni was my opposite in that regard, but it was probably why our friendship worked so well. We balanced each other out. Without her, I'd never leave the house. Without me, she'd have jumped off a bridge because she heard that someone else had done it.

"I don't know about this," I said. "Maybe we should wait."

"We're not doing anything," she insisted. "Just driving by."

But I knew her. She'd never be satisfied with "just" driving by. She was only saying that so I wouldn't chicken out. My fingers started to tremble as we turned left onto a residential road.

I put my hands under my thighs. "How much longer?"

Toni peeked at the GPS app on her phone. "We're here."

I swallowed hard as the car rolled to a stop. My eyes traveled up a long driveway to a magnificent white house with three pillars at the center. My breath caught in my throat. Flynn—of the ratty trench coat and beat-up jeans—and this place? The two did not match.

"It looks like your not-so-dead boyfriend is loaded," Toni said.

"Evan and Flynn *have* to be two different people," I said quickly.

She grinned mischievously. "There's only one way to find out . . ."

My stomach turned. I imagined myself strutting up to the door and banging my fist. What if his parents opened it? What if Evan was Flynn? What if he wasn't? I wasn't ready for this. I had to have a plan in case the boys were one and the same. And I needed a fake reason to talk to Evan in case they weren't. This was moving too fast.

But here was an opportunity, staring me in the face. Should I really pass it up to wait for a more perfect moment?

I turned away from the house and rubbed my temples.

Toni craned her neck. "The property is gated, but it looks like there's an intercom button. We could pretend to be someone else."

She was already thinking logistics while I was still trying to talk myself into it.

She let out a grunt of annoyance. "There's no way to see if anyone's home or not. There's nothing in the driveway, but they have a three-car garage. Wait . . . someone's coming down the street . . ."

I looked up and saw another vehicle coming from the opposite direction. It rolled to an almost-stop, like they, too, were spying on the big house. Time seemed to slow. And then, after a moment's hesitation, the engine roared back to life and it sped on.

"That was weird," Toni said.

But I couldn't respond. A trembling spread from my hands through my entire body.

It was a black SUV.

Exactly like the one that had killed Flynn.

CHAPTER 6
CHAPTER 6
CHAPTER 6
CHAPTER 6

CHAPTER 6

"So I realize I may have pushed you too far yesterday," Toni said at lunch the next day.

We sat at our usual table, the long one by the back wall, as far from the stench of steamed hot dogs as we could get. The same fading posters had hung on the wall for years, featuring past-their-prime celebrities reminding us to drink our milk. And a fluorescent light flickered and buzzed above us in its final death throes before burnout.

I stabbed my salad with a plastic fork. "Whatever gave you that idea? My near-panic attack?"

"Yeah, green's not your color, girl." Her voice softened. "Are you feeling better today?"

After I'd seen the black SUV, I'd had a minor freakout and demanded that Toni drive us home. Along the way I explained why, shuddering at the memory of Flynn's body in the road. She listened and sympathized, but also tried to talk some sense into me. Black SUVs were everywhere. Just because one slowed down in front of Evan/Flynn's house, that didn't mean anything.

"I'm fine," I said to her now. "Thanks to you, Miss Voice of Reason."

Brigid sat down beside me and ripped the top off her yogurt. "I don't think I've ever heard Toni accused of being a voice of reason before. Do tell."

I froze. I still wasn't ready to explain any of this to our other friends.

"It's only for a history project," Toni said. "Nothing exciting. And I'm sure Morgan will never use such slanderous words in reference to me again."

I forced a laugh. "So, Brigid. It's Friday. Tell us what's going on this weekend." I figured if anything could slide Brigid toward a different conversation, it would be an offer to plan my social calendar.

Predictably, she brightened. "Reece is having another flashlight party tomorrow night! We should go."

The last place I wanted to go was a party. I wanted to sit at home with my friend Google and try to figure this thing out.

But Toni shot up straight in her seat. "Yes! Morgan, we should totally go to Reece's party. He has *cute* friends."

Cute friends? What was she . . . *Oh.*

"Hey, Morgan." Jennifer tapped me on the shoulder. She had a checklist in her hand. This usually meant work, but I had nowhere to hide.

"What's up, Jennifer?" I asked.

48   K.A. HARRINGTON

"Do you have all the team photos shot yet? We're about to hit our deadline."

Jennifer was the editor in chief of our school yearbook. I took a lot of photos for them. Even though it didn't pay, it was something I could put on my college applications.

"I did all the teams except baseball," I said.

Brigid snorted, and Toni burst into laughter.

"Really, guys?" I said, though I was giggling, too. "Get your minds out of the gutter."

Jennifer tapped her list impatiently. "Can you do the baseball team this afternoon?"

Toni nearly fell off her chair.

"Yes, I will take a team *photo* of the baseball guys after school," I said, glaring at Toni.

Jennifer left to bug the next person on her list. I was expecting another joke from Toni, but she'd turned serious.

"Reece is on the baseball team," she said.

"So?" Brigid asked.

Toni looked right at me. "So Morgan could find out if any of his cute friends are coming to the party . . ."

Luckily, the baseball team had a home game that afternoon, so they were in their uniforms. The coach told me I had five minutes to assemble them and get my picture before they had to be on the field. But it was like trying to round up bees. One would get a call on his cell and then two more would wander off in conversation.

"Guys!" I yelled. "Come on. Just give me ten seconds and then you can go."

I tried to corral them in some kind of order—tallest standing in the back, shortest in the middle row, late people on their knees in the front. I took another step back to fit everyone in the frame. Perfect. *Click.*

"Wait!" Another straggler ran up.

I didn't even try to hide my sigh of aggravation. "Kneel down in the front row."

I refocused and tried again. *Click, click, click.*

I looked down at the display. New Guy had dropped his equipment bag on the ground, and part of it was in the shot. "One more," I said.

"Enough!" the coach growled. "We have to warm up for the game. Now."

I took a deep breath. In most areas of my life I was far from a perfectionist, but I took my photographs seriously. Especially the ones I took on my own, for my abandoned-places series. The yearbook photos didn't have soul, but that didn't mean I wanted them to look sloppy.

It seemed I had no choice, though. I had only one minute left as the team grabbed their equipment, and I knew how I had to spend it.

"Reece!" I called, jogging up to him.

He pulled a brown leather baseball glove out of his bag and straightened. "Yeah?"

I lowered my voice. "You're having another flashlight party Saturday night?"

He smiled as he glanced left and right. "Yeah," he whispered. "I'll send out a text chain with the address around eight that night. Are you and Toni coming?"

I noticed the hopeful edge to his question. "That depends," I answered.

He gave me a wary look. "On what?"

"Can you get your friend Evan Murphy to come?"

"Does Morgan have an online crush?" he teased with a wry smirk.

I crossed my arms. "Can you get him to come or not?"

He sighed. "I haven't seen that guy in two years."

"So it's time to catch up," I suggested.

Reece shook his head. "I don't usually invite random dudes on FriendShare to my parties." But then he paused. "How about a trade? I'll get Evan to come to the party . . . if you get Toni to go on a date with me."

I opened my mouth, closed it, then opened it again. "Well, um, yeah, you can hang with her at the party."

"No. A date."

"I don't think she'd be interested," I said quickly.

"Just dinner."

"I'm sorry, Reece. I think you're out of luck."

He shrugged. "Then so are you."

"I'm not a prostitute!" Toni yelled. We were sitting in my room later that afternoon, listening to music, our books spread out on the floor around us.

"It's just dinner," I said. "He'll take you to Macaroni's. You can get your favorite chicken parm."

"I'm not a chicken parm prostitute either!"

"Please. I'll . . . I'll even come with you. We'll negotiate that into the deal." I pressed my hands together and gave her a pitifully desperate look. "I just really need Reece to get Evan to this party. I need to see him with my own eyes."

Toni groaned and tossed an eraser at my face. "I'm the bestest best friend you'll ever have. Better than best."

"You are."

"And I'm getting dessert."

"Two if you like."

"And I now have a 'you owe me one' that will never expire, to use at my discretion."

"Okay, maybe I'm starting to regret this."

She launched a notebook at my head.

The houses on my road were all the same—medium-sized colonials, in shades of white and beige, with attached one-car garages. When giving directions, we clung to whatever identifying characteristics we could. The one after the one with the basketball hoop in the driveway. The one with the rosebush by the front door.

I kind of preferred Toni's street. The houses weren't all built at the same time and the styles varied. There was a split-level next to a sprawling ranch next to a Victorian. Toni's house was a pretty ranch with an in-ground pool and a huge backyard. Toni, Cooper, and I had spent so many summer afternoons playing wiffle ball in that yard, until we were covered in sweat, and then cannonballing into the pool, squealing and laughing. But last summer the pool needed a repair, and that particular expense was not high on the priority list. The cover stayed on, collecting leaves and small puddles of dirty water.

I got to Toni's house after dinner Saturday, with plenty of time to get ready for the party together. I parked in the driveway and walked toward the front door. A weather-beaten For Sale sign stood crookedly in their front yard, the same place it had been for the past year. But Toni said it was hopeless. The house was worth only half of what her parents had paid for it. So even if someone actually wanted to move *into* River's End, their offer would never be enough for her parents to pay off the loan and get a new place somewhere else. Plus, there were always more than fifty other houses for sale in town as well. At first, Toni had been worried about moving to another town. Now she worried about worse things—like the bank taking the house.

I raised my hand to knock, but before I had a chance, the door whipped open. I backed up a step, my fist still in the air. Cooper, holding a finger to his lips, pulled me inside and closed the door behind us. My eyes took in the mess of the living room. Papers were tossed on the floor. Mr. Klane was asleep on the sofa, one hand dangling off the cushion. A short glass sat on the coffee table, filled with something that looked like apple juice but surely wasn't. A smash came from the kitchen.

"Mom's still pissed about a fight they had earlier," Cooper whispered. "Can you drive to the party? I don't want to leave a car there. Diana's coming, and we're going to spend the night back at her dorm."

"She's coming to the party?" I asked, surprised. Ever since she graduated, Cooper's girlfriend acted like she was too good for River's End.

"Of course not," Cooper said. "She's just picking me up."

That made more sense.

"It hasn't been the best day here. Um, can you make sure Toni . . ." He looked around, like he didn't want anyone to hear.

"I'll have her sleep at my house tonight."

He let out a sigh of relief. "Thanks."

My heart went out to him. He was so protective of his little sister. He never wanted to leave her home alone when things were exploding between their parents. I often wondered what would happen in the fall when he was gone for good.

A shuffling of footsteps came from the kitchen. "Oh, it's *you*," Mrs. Klane said. There was a strange edge to her tone. She leaned against the doorway, looking me over. "How are your parents?"

The question was innocent enough, but there was an undercurrent to it that made me uncomfortable. "They're fine," I said. "Thanks for asking."

She wordlessly returned to the kitchen and loudly threw something into the sink.

When Toni and I were little, our parents were coworkers and best friends. After Stell went down, so did their friendship. At first, things drifted to a polite civility when dropping Toni off, or vice versa. Then, when Toni and I were old enough to arrange our own playdates, our families just ignored each other. My parents seemed wary of Toni's. I knew it was the alcohol. They mentioned that they didn't like me "in that environment." And it was obvious that Toni's parents held some bitterness against mine as well. Maybe because my family still had our heads above water?

Cooper led me down the hallway toward Toni's room.

Toni's door cracked open, and she poked her face out. "I thought I heard you," she said, and waved me inside.

I glanced over my shoulder as Cooper retreated into his bedroom.

Toni closed the door behind us. Her room smelled like nail

polish and perfume. As usual, her bed was made, her desk chair pushed in, books neatly stacked. Even her shoes were perfectly lined up at the bottom of her closet, two by two. Her room was always clean and organized, in stark contrast to the rest of the house.

She pressed a button on the speaker and turned on some music, an old Florence + The Machine song. She bopped around the room, singing the lyrics. Her dad was passed out on the couch and her mom was smashing things in the kitchen, but apparently she didn't want to talk about it. And that was fine.

I glanced down at my phone and scrolled through the text messages. No address for the party yet.

"How do The Pointer Sisters look?" Toni asked.

That was what she lovingly called her boobs. Toni wasn't just petite, she was small in every way. She needed a size A-*minus* bra, but since they didn't make those, she just bought the kind that pushes what little you have up and together.

"They look great," I said, keeping my eyes on my phone.

"You didn't even look."

I glanced up. Toni had her hands on her hips, pouting. She wore black pants, a tight red top, and heels that brought her up to five foot three.

"They look fantastic. Boobalicious."

"What are you wearing?" she asked.

I slid the phone into my back pocket and struck a model pose. "This."

Toni looked at me like one of my limbs had just fallen off. "You can't be serious."

I looked down at my jeans-and-hoodie ensemble. "I'm not going to this party to pick up a new guy. I'm going so I can find out if my old one is actually dead."

"And don't you want to look your best in that 'gotcha' moment?"

She had a point. What I'd pictured in my head was me screaming at Flynn, *How could you do this? How could you let me go on thinking you were dead?* But it couldn't hurt to make him wince at what he'd left behind.

She saw my change in expression and said, "Leave it up to me."

After tossing her closet like she had a search warrant, Toni finally picked out an outfit and laid it on the bed.

"That's for me?" I asked.

"Yep!"

"Nope." I shook my head.

Toni scowled. "You agreed."

I picked up the tight black skirt and held it over my jeans. "I think you're forgetting about our height difference. This is a mini on you. It'll be illegal on me."

"How about just the tank?" She held up a shimmering violet tank top. "It'll look great with your jeans."

"Deal." I'd have preferred something warmer, but it was best to quit while I was ahead.

I put the tank on, and my phone buzzed.

14 Meadow Place.

I drew in a shaky breath. "Here we go."

CHAPTER 7
CHAPTER 7
CHAPTER 7
CHAPTER 7

CHAPTER 7

I never told anyone that Flynn broke up with me the night he was killed. Not even Toni. I couldn't count how many times I'd rerun that night in my head. If I'd changed only one thing, Flynn would be alive. If I'd stayed home. If I hadn't seen him on the way to the party and pulled over. If we hadn't fought in the car. If he hadn't dumped me and started walking. If I'd driven slower or faster. Any one of these things and the black SUV would've raced down the street without barreling into him.

But I never shared those feelings with anyone. Toni would just yell at me and say I shouldn't feel guilty. But just because I *shouldn't* didn't mean I wouldn't.

As I drove toward Meadow Place with Toni riding shotgun and Cooper in the back, I thought about what I wanted to happen at this party. Did I want Evan to be Flynn? If he was, then that meant he'd let me believe he was dead. He'd done this cruel thing without even a thought to how much it would hurt me. But if Evan *wasn't* Flynn . . . then Flynn was still dead. And I'd spend more hours lying awake, changing minute details of that night in a futile attempt to save Flynn's life, if only in my mind.

There was no positive outcome.

And, even though Reece invited him, there was no guarantee that the kid would even show up. If he *was* Flynn, he might be worried that I'd be at the party. Or Toni, or one or two of my other friends who'd met him while we were dating. I could be doing all this worrying and he might not even come. I tightened my grip on the steering wheel.

"Why are you guys so quiet?" Cooper called out from the back.

"I just love this song," I said, turning up the volume. I didn't even know the song. I just couldn't make small talk while my mind was racing.

I slowed as we got near the road. Right before Stell had gone under, the plan for Meadow Place had been another development of McMansions. The developer stopped building after people stopped buying. A few lots only had foundations filled. A couple had frames. And the rest were almost finished—some even had their walls painted and hardwood floors inserted. But none of them ever sold, and they weren't even really for sale now, so they didn't have electricity or heat turned on.

When Reece organized these parties, he did his best to keep them under the radar. He never allowed people to trash the places and always cleaned up afterward. He cased empty houses, found one that had an unlocked window or an easy-to-pick lock, and started planning. He released the address to others at party time. It spread out in a text chain, and within minutes everyone knew where to go. Even though the neighborhood was deserted, Reece always hung light-blocking curtains in any windows, and we parked on an adjacent road so the cars wouldn't attract attention.

I parked on a quiet side street behind some other cars I recognized from school. We each grabbed a flashlight, but kept them off. The rule was no lights until we were inside. We walked up to house fourteen, a large cream-colored colonial. I couldn't even hear the music until we were at the front door.

This was really happening. A drop of cold sweat trickled down my back. I'd wanted to have a speech ready. A great one-liner to throw in his face. Something that told him how angry I was, how hurt I felt. I needed to know how he could've done something so awful. But the words wouldn't arrange themselves in my head.

"What are you waiting for?" Cooper asked, then reached around me and pushed the door open.

Toni pulled me inside and closed the door behind us. The house had finished walls and hardwoods, plus an open floor plan from what would've been a kitchen into the dining and living rooms. A few battery-operated camping lanterns were placed strategically throughout. And, in addition, almost everyone had their own flashlight. I'd been to only a couple of these parties, but they were all the same. In the early hours people mostly stood around and talked. But by the end, people lost themselves in the music and the dancing lights.

We worked our way through the kitchen first. The house had no furniture. Counter space was premium seating. If you were lucky enough to grab a spot, you didn't dare take a bathroom break, because your seat would be taken by the time you got back. A couple of groups were sitting on the floor in the large living room, but most people stood. No dancing yet.

"See him?" Toni whispered into my ear.

I squinted at the crowd. "No. But the light is so dim. I need to find Reece. He'll know if he's here."

"I'll walk around, do some reconnaissance," she said, wagging her eyebrows.

"Want a drink?" Cooper yelled over the music.

"No, thanks," I said, watching Toni disappear into the crowd.

A senior I recognized leaned toward Cooper. "Hey, who's the blond shortie?"

"My sister," Cooper growled. "And if you even *think* about her, I'll murder you in your sleep."

The guy backed off, hands held up. "All right, then."

I snickered. Toni would kill Cooper if she knew how often he did that. But I'd never tell.

I recognized Reece's overstyled hair as he walked by. I tapped his shoulder. "Hey Reece, is Evan here?"

He whistled. "Wow, you just get right down to it, huh? All

this from a FriendShare photo? I mean, he's a good-enough-looking guy, but—"

"Reece," I interrupted. "Is he here or not?"

He scanned the room for a moment. "I don't think he's here yet."

I gritted my teeth. "You promised."

"Relax." He put a hand on my shoulder. "He'll show. Go have a good time."

I wandered into the living room. Electronic music pumped from a speaker and a few people had started to dance, waving their flashlights above their heads. I leaned my back against the nearest wall and watched the dizzying patterns of lights on the ceiling. They seemed to pulse with the music.

Even with no heat, the air in the house felt humid. I was glad Toni had made me wear the tank top after all. After a few minutes, she rejoined me.

"Having fun holding up this wall?" she teased.

"I can't just walk around and make small talk," I said. "Not when he could come in that door at any moment."

"How about I talk to keep your mind off it? Would that help?"

I nodded, but my eyes were still scanning the crowd.

Toni examined her manicure. "Let's see. Well, Reece told me how much he was looking forward to our date, and I asked him if he'd mind wearing a paper bag over his head with a picture of Ian Somerhalder glued onto it. Amy is making out with

Jacob in the corner, so I guess they didn't stay broken up for long. Diana is coming to get Cooper, but she won't deign to come inside, so she's going to text him when she's here. How obnoxious is that? I mean, she only graduated a few months ago. She couldn't come in for one second?"

"Totally agree," I said.

The front door opened, and my breath caught in my throat. But it was only Nikki Trotto. She did a slow walk through the room. "Hey, girls," she said, looking us up and down in her pinched-nose judgy way.

"Hey, Nikki," Toni unenthusiastically replied.

Modeling herself after reality-show girls, Nikki had adopted a nickname. She told everyone that people called her Sikki because her body was so "sick." But we all knew she gave the nickname to herself. And even in the dim light, she still looked like she'd taken a bath in Cheetos.

"Bronzer much?" Toni whispered, and I held back a laugh.

I had to admit, Toni's mindless gossip was actually helping to calm me down. I could already feel some of the tension release from my shoulders. I closed my eyes and did a slow neck roll.

"Boo," someone said in my ear. My eyes snapped open, but a blinding light forced them closed again.

"Stop it," Toni said, and then I heard a smacking sound.

After a moment, I could see again. It was Reece. Though Toni had wrestled away his flashlight.

"I'm only fooling around," he said, sounding sufficiently chastised.

"What do you want?" I said.

He pointed toward the kitchen. "He's here."

My lungs seized.

I followed the line of his finger to a tall guy standing alone against a wall. He wore a red baseball hat, same as in his FriendShare profile picture, but the bill hung low over his face. I couldn't see his features from this distance.

Reece grabbed his flashlight back and wandered into the crowd.

"Want me to walk by first?" Toni asked. "Get a look?"

I nodded, barely able to get a word out.

Toni sauntered by him and giggled as she playfully grabbed the hat off his head. Then she disappeared around the corner. I watched as he raised his hands in the air, wondering what had just happened. Within seconds Toni snuck up behind me.

Like I said. Ninja.

"I think it's Flynn," she breathed at my back. "It's *almost* him . . . but I don't know." She paused. "You would know better than me."

I had to approach him. This was the moment. I took a deep breath and silently told my nerves to calm the hell down. I couldn't freak out and blow it now.

I pushed my way through the crowd, my eyes never leaving the back of his head. I crept up behind him. His frame was the same—the broad shoulders, the height. I reached my hand out and held it in the air above his shoulder. So close. All I had to do was touch him and he'd turn around.

But suddenly I had a better idea. Thanks to Reece.

I quickly spun around to his front and held my flashlight up to his face, so I could examine him but he couldn't see me.

His hair was short, brown rather than black, but that could've been easily changed with nine bucks and a box of dye. I searched his face and immediately recognized features. Those gray eyes, pale as ice, his strong nose, the jawline I'd laid a trail of kisses along.

My heart hammered in my chest.

He winced. "What's with the light in the eyes?" he said, and let out a nervous laugh.

And that's when I saw it.

As he smiled, a dimple formed in his left cheek. It was a great smile—half-cocky, half-adorable—but it wasn't Flynn's. You can't hide a dimple, and I'd seen Flynn smile enough times to know he didn't have one.

Evan looked a hell of a lot like Flynn, but he wasn't him.

I brought the flashlight back down to my side. Evan blinked quickly as his eyes readjusted. And then he saw *me* for the first time.

He opened his mouth to speak, but stopped. His eyes flashed with what looked like recognition and then widened with something unexpected. Fear.

He mumbled something I couldn't hear and walked away. I stood for a moment, stunned. He wasn't Flynn. I was sure of that. I didn't know this boy.

But he knew me.

With a jolt, I regained the use of my muscles. I dashed into the living room, but everyone was dancing now, and the spinning flashlights made it impossible for me to pick out his face. I ran down the hall and checked the bathroom—empty. I circled back to the kitchen and frantically looked from tall guy to tall guy.

Someone grabbed my arm.

"Hey," Reece said. "What did you say to Evan?"

"I didn't say anything. Why?"

Reece let me go and gave me a skeptical look. "It was weird. He ran up to me, pointed you out, and asked who you were. I told him your name and he took off. What the hell did you do? Try to jump him? Down, girl," he said, laughing.

I groaned and shook my head. "So he just . . . left?"

"Yeah." Reece turned uncharacteristically serious for a moment. "Morgan, he seemed . . . spooked. Why would he be scared of *you*?"

CHAPTER 8

"Thanks for leaving early with me," I said to Toni later that night in my bedroom. I'd changed into my pajamas and washed my face, though I was nowhere near ready for sleep. My mind was still racing.

Toni had changed, too, and was now sitting up in bed scrolling through FriendShare on her phone. "No problem," she said, dropping the phone onto her lap. "I mean, I would've been freaked out, too."

I slumped into my desk chair. "What do you think it means, that he knows me?"

"He didn't know you," Toni said. "He asked Reece who you were."

"Yeah, but he recognized me. I saw it in his face. And Reece said he seemed afraid of me."

Toni gave me a look. "Well, you did ambush him and blast your flashlight in his eyes. And some other girl had just stolen his hat."

I hadn't thought of it that way. Was it possible that he hadn't recognized me at all? He was just . . . wigged out? There he was, at a party where he didn't know anyone but some random dude from FriendShare, then one girl runs off with his hat and another blinds him with a flashlight. Maybe he was just annoyed and left. Maybe the rest was all in my head.

"How do you feel about scrounging up some snackage for us?" Toni asked.

That was the least I could do after freaking out. "Salty or sweet?"

"Surprise me!"

I tossed her the remote for the small television that sat on top of my dresser. "Your job is to find something good for us to watch."

I tiptoed downstairs, the plush carpet scuffing against my slippers. My parents were awake when we got home, but they'd be asleep by now. As I got to the bottom step, though, I paused. There were voices in the kitchen.

I held my breath and listened. I stood still and tried to make out some of the words. I didn't usually sneak around eavesdropping on my parents, but something about their tone made me hesitate. It was hushed. Secretive. They wouldn't be worried about waking me and Toni up. They knew we stayed up half the night when we were together. So the only other answer was that they were talking about something they didn't want me to overhear.

I crept along the wall and moved silently through the living room, avoiding the open doorway that led to the kitchen. Closer now, I could hear them better.

"I just don't think the time is right," my dad said.

"Noah, I'm starting to think you'll never find a right time," my mom snapped.

Her tone shocked me. Just because my parents never fought in front of me, I wasn't naïve enough to think that they never fought at all. But still, it was shocking to hear them talk to each other this way.

"Consider that for a moment," Dad said.

"Consider what?"

"That maybe she doesn't ever need to know."

She? She who? Me? I slid along the wall, trying to get as close as I could to the doorway.

"But what if she finds out from someone else?" Mom said. "Have you thought through the repercussions of that? I think it should come from us."

I strained to listen. I was barely breathing. If I could've momentarily stopped my heart from beating to hear better, I would have. I took one more step and put my hand up against the wall for balance. But it wasn't the wall, it was the light switch. And apparently my flannel pj's, slippers, and slow shuffle across the carpet had created a perfect storm. The biggest static electricity shock I'd ever gotten shot out from the light switch to my hand. I saw blue.

And . . . I yelled.

Chairs screeched as both my parents jumped up from the kitchen table. They appeared in the doorway a moment later, looking concerned as I cradled my electrocuted hand.

"What happened?" Mom asked.

"Um, I came down for some snacks, and I went to hit the light switch and got shocked."

Now that it was clear I wasn't really hurt, my dad laughed. "It's those stupid slippers." He pointed down at my favorite bunny slippers. They were so old, the bottoms were nearly worn through. "You have to throw those things out."

"Never!" I battle-cried and shuffled forward on the carpet to recharge. Then I reached out my hand like a weapon.

He backed up a step, and I swiped at the air. "Missed me!" he called, and then ran up the stairs like a kid.

I smiled. Dad and I had waged static electricity wars before. Neither of us had outgrown them yet, obviously. It had even almost made me forget the conversation I'd walked in on. Almost, but not quite.

Mom went into the kitchen and took two mugs off the table and placed them in the sink.

"You guys are up late," I pointed out, eyeing the cups.

She wiped her hands on a dish towel and smiled. "Heading up now."

I hesitated for a moment. "What were you talking about?"

Her smile faltered. "A lot of things. Why?"

It felt like we were playing a game. And for some reason I didn't want to show all my cards. "I thought I heard something about me, maybe."

She turned away and opened a cabinet. She pulled out a yellow bag and pressed it into my hands. "Sour Patch Kids," she said. "Toni's favorite, right?"

I nodded and kneaded the bag of candy with my fingers. Whatever the conversation had been about, Mom wanted me to let it go. But I couldn't. I had to try one more time. I took a step forward, closing the distance between us. "Is there something I need to know, Mom?"

Her eyes darted to the doorway and back at me. "You were at Toni's house earlier tonight, right?"

"Yeah. We got ready for the party there."

"I'd prefer it if you did that here," she said matter-of-factly.

I gave her a questioning look. "Huh?"

Mom lowered her voice. "The Klanes are kind of a mess right now. I'm sure you know that. And your father and I just . . . don't want you in that environment."

She reached out and gently tucked a strand of my hair behind my ear. "You know we love Toni," she said. "She's welcome here anytime."

Before I could formulate any follow-up questions, Mom brushed by me and went upstairs. Clutching the bag of candy in my hand, I thought about her explanation. Could that be it? They'd only been talking about not wanting me at Toni's house? That wasn't exactly a big secret.

I couldn't shake the feeling that there was something more.

CHAPTER 9

"I'm going to kill you."

I closed my locker door Monday afternoon and found Toni standing beside me. Even with her arms crossed and an angry scowl on her face, she wasn't intimidating. I think there's a rule that you have to be over five feet tall to be intimidating.

"You know how many times Reece has mentioned our 'date' today?" She used finger-quotes as she said the word.

"Two?" I said hopefully.

"Try six. Plus he told the entire school. I've had people coming up to me all day asking about it."

I smiled sheepishly. "Did you use a different shampoo today? Your hair looks even shinier than normal. And you smell pretty."

She put her hand up. "There aren't enough fake compliments in the world, Morgan."

I batted my eyelashes and made a pouty face. "How can I make it up to you?"

"You can—and *will*—come with me on this godforsaken date from hell. And you won't complain about whichever tool friend of his you get stuck with."

A double date was the last thing I wanted to do. But I had no plans Friday, no excuse, and I owed it to her. "Deal."

"You're damn right," she said, and sashayed away.

I had just finished packing up my equipment from Photography Club after school on Wednesday when Reece strolled in.

"Morgan Tulley. What. Issss. Uuuup."

He couldn't just say hi. He had to talk like a DJ who'd had one too many Red Bulls. "Hey, Reece."

"Whatcha doin'?"

"Photography Club just let out. I'm organizing my files." I clicked to close my photo of a vandalized wall, then closed my folder.

"Any nude selfies in there?"

I let out an annoyed sigh. "Really, Reece?"

He laughed. "Come on. You know I'm just joking around." He settled into the seat beside me. "So what does the Photography Club do?"

I raised an eyebrow. Surely he wasn't here for small talk, but I humored him. "Sometimes we have a prompt and we take photos based on that. Sometimes Mr. Durant, our adviser, works with us on the technicals. Sometimes we work on a concept. We critique each other." I shrugged. "Lots of stuff."

He gestured toward the now dark screen of the monitor. "Are you compiling your pics to enter them in a contest or something?"

"I'm working on my portfolio."

"Do you specialize in anything? Faces . . . bowls of fruit . . . your hot friends . . ."

I pulled my backpack up onto my lap. A blatant hint that I was ready for this awkward conversation to end. "Abandoned places."

He gave me a mysterious smile. "Like Happy Time Mini Golf?"

"Yeah . . . ," I said warily. "I haven't shot there yet, but I'm planning to, actually."

"Hmm." He tapped on his chin.

I narrowed my eyes. "Reece, what do you really want?"

"Okay, so you know I'm taking Toni out on a date Friday night?"

"Right . . ."

He rubbed his palms together, apparently nearing the point of all of this. "Do you have any, like, tips?"

"On what?"

"Impressing Toni."

I burst out laughing. "Reece, I'm not going to try to help you get into my best friend's pants."

He groaned. "It's not like that, Morgan. I really like her. She's different."

"You're just interested because she's the only girl who doesn't fall for your cool-guy act."

"Not true. You don't buy my shit either, but I'm not after *you*."

My mouth opened.

He held his hands up. "Sorry. No offense."

"None taken. Listen, Reece. You're just not her type."

"So help me *become* her type. I've had a mad crush on the girl since the fourth grade. She's just so cute and funny and . . ." He stopped, looking embarrassed. "I know she's not taking this date thing seriously, but I want her to give me a chance. A real one. Come on. Help a bro out."

His eyes were so sincere that I actually felt bad for him. "Tips. Okay."

"Be totally honest."

Well, you asked for it. "Okay, first off," I said, "don't dress like a doucheface."

His mouth dropped open. "What does that even mean?"

"She doesn't like guys who dress like they're going to a club. Leave the tight shirt at home."

He nodded. "Okay, that's a good tip. What else?"

"Don't be yourself."

He balked. "What the hell, Morgan?"

"You told me to be honest!"

"Fine. Fine." He ran a hand through his spiky hair. "Explain."

"You know how you are . . . with the swagger and the over-confidence. Just stop. Be a regular person."

"Like . . . a nice guy?" He said it like it was a fatal diagnosis.

"Yes. Some girls like nice guys. You'd be surprised."

He took a deep breath. "Anything else?"

"That's a good enough start. Also, don't douse yourself in cologne."

"I get it. I get it. Sheesh."

"You wanted to know," I said, standing up.

He stopped me. "Wait, there's one more thing." He had this silly grin on his face that filled me with suspicion. "Toni said you wanted to come along, too. Make it a double-date thing."

"*Want* isn't the word I would've used."

He let out a giant sigh. "She's forcing you. I figured that much out. But it actually works out well."

"Why is that?"

"Turns out the guy I'm helping you stalk is interested right back."

I shook my head quickly. "What are you talking about?"

"Evan."

Evan was . . . interested? A thousand questions churned in my head. "Did he contact you?"

"Yeah. He wanted to know more about you." He whispered conspiratorially, "Don't worry. I didn't tell him you were a crazy stalker."

"I'm not!"

Reece waved his hand. "Whatever. I didn't tell him anything about you making sure he was at the party and all that."

Well, that was good, but . . . "What *did* you tell him?"

He shrugged. "That you're a cool chick and that you're single."

"And what did he say?"

"He wanted to know if I could arrange a way for you to end up in the same place together. So he could get to know you better. So I invited him along Friday night."

I stared at a poster on the wall, just over Reece's shoulder. But I wasn't really seeing it. I was trying to figure this out in my head. It made no sense. Were my initial instincts correct after all? Did Evan know me? If so, how? And why did he have such a weird first reaction?

"Morgan!" Reece snapped his fingers in front of my face. "Do you get what I'm saying? Dreamboy Evan is your date Friday night. Aren't you happy?"

I forced my mouth to work. "Yeah. I am. Thanks."

He smiled as he stood to leave. "It was so strange. I was thinking, you know, first you ask me to secretly hook you up with Evan. And then Evan asks me to hook him up with you. Not sure how I wound up being the middleman, but it's like you guys are weirdly meant to be."

CHAPTER 10
CHAPTER 10
CHAPTER 10
CHAPTER 10

CHAPTER 10

Friday night, we took Wingate Road from the center of town. Reece drove, with Toni in the passenger seat and me—the third wheel—in the back.

"I offered to pick Evan up," Reece said as we stopped at a light. "But he said he'd meet us there. I think he's still scared of you."

Toni chuckled.

"Very funny." I crossed my arms and looked out the window. "Where are we going anyway?"

Reece's eyes flicked to mine in the rearview. "Happy Time Mini Golf."

"Awesome!" Toni turned in her seat. "You've been wanting to go there. Do you have your camera with you?"

"No, but I can plan out some shots." I smiled. Reece had chosen the place specifically because he knew I'd like it. Maybe he wasn't so bad.

"See that beauty up there?" Reece let up on the gas and slowed past a house up on a hill, surrounded by a black iron gate. We had a lot of nice houses in town, but this one was even bigger. It reminded me of Evan's house in Littlefield. "Some night we'll party there. It's the King Mother of houses."

"King Mother is a contradiction," Toni said.

Reece gave her a playful look. "Fine, it's the Queen Mother. No one lives there right now, I think, so I doubt there's a security system. But that gate around the property is locked, and there's no side street nearby to easily hide all the cars. One of these days, though, I'll figure out the best way to conquer it. And we will party!"

Toni snorted. "Such lofty ambition you have. And to think some people want to cure cancer."

"There will be plenty of time for that once I get out of River's End," Reece said. "But for now . . . a guy's got to have a short-term goal."

I had to hand it to him, Reece was good at organizing. He worked with what we had. City kids had rooftop parties. Country kids took over barns. We had empty places.

Minutes later we parked in the lot for Happy Time Mini Golf. I twisted in my seat to quickly take in every corner. No sign of Evan.

"He'll be here," Reece said, reading my mind. "I'm going to get the stuff ready."

He got out and popped the trunk. Toni reached for the door handle, but I put my hand on her shoulder and said, "Wait a sec."

"Don't worry," she said, turning to face me. "I'm here. So if the guy's a weirdo, we can just—"

"It's not that," I interrupted. "It's Reece."

"We already know *he's* a weirdo."

"No. Just . . ." I sighed. "I know this isn't a real date and you're not into it, but do me a favor and be nice to him."

Toni rolled her eyes. "Jeez, Morgan. Did you think I was going to be rude all night? I'm not a stone-cold bitch, just a room-temperature one."

"I know. It's just . . . he's actually not that bad. Keep an open mind."

She looked at me like I'd sprouted a second head. "Focus on your own fake date and I'll worry about mine."

"Heads up!" Reece called from outside.

A plain, gray sedan pulled into the lot and parked beside us. My muscles tensed as I saw Evan behind the wheel. Knowing the size of the house this guy lived in, I'd been expecting him to drive something a little more flashy. But I was kind of glad that he didn't. He killed the engine and got out, wearing jeans and a black fleece jacket.

"Time to go!" Toni said, and bounded out of the car.

I followed wordlessly, my throat feeling suddenly tight. I had no idea why Evan wanted to see me again. I kept my eyes on the pavement as I stepped toward him, admiring the hardy weeds that pushed through the cracks. When I was close enough to see the cuffs of his dark jeans, I looked up.

I had to hold back the gasp that wanted to escape from my mouth. *Flynn's cheekbones, Flynn's nose, Flynn's mouth.* Memories flashed in my mind. I tried to focus on the differences. Evan's hair: shorter and a lighter shade than Flynn's. His eyes: the same color as Flynn's, but these seemed to hold more life in them. More curiosity. And there was that dimple.

"Hey," he said with a cautious smile.

"Hey," I said back.

This was . . . awkward. *Do we shake hands or what?*

He stuffed his hands in the pockets of his fleece, taking away that option. But then he took a step closer. Just one. Like he was testing the waters. And he never for a second took his eyes off mine. Like he was waiting for me to do something. What, I didn't know.

Well, two could play this game. I could act just as standoffish. I stood mutely, never breaking my stare.

"I'm Evan," he said, ending the silence.

"Morgan."

The way he watched me made me feel like a display in a museum. Like he was trying to figure me out, see into my head.

I stared back.

Toni cleared her throat. "Okay, this isn't weird at all."

"Yeah, let's play." Reece pointed at the sky. "We only have an hour until the sun sets."

As if suddenly remembering there were two other people here, Evan looked around. "Why did we meet *here*?"

Reece patted him on the back. "I figured we'd let our out-of-towner experience one of River's End's traditional pastimes. Welcome to Happy Time Mini Golf."

Evan gave us a puzzled look and pointed at the giant sign that said, For Sale or Lease Commercial Property. "It's closed."

"Don't worry." Reece walked back to the trunk. "I've got that covered." He pulled out four golf clubs and a plastic bag with a bunch of balls. He held a club out to Evan. "Welcome to River's End. Where *everything's* closed."

Evan looked at each of us in turn and grinned. "So you just bring your own clubs and play?"

"Yep," Toni said. "No one cares."

"The clubs are my dad's," Reece explained. "The balls are all white, so we have to play through each hole one by one. But it's free and we have the place to ourselves."

Evan nodded, looking impressed. Toni grabbed the bag from Reece and started looking through it. Even though all the balls were the same, she wanted to choose hers.

I looked back at Evan and caught him staring at me. "Have you ever done this before?" I asked. "A blind date?"

With a sly smile, he said, "*Is* it blind?"

"Well, I don't know *you*," I said, filling the last word with meaning.

"But you came up to *me* at the party."

"And *you* ran away."

His eyes flashed in amusement. Part of me had expected

him to have Flynn's voice—the lips were the same. But Evan's voice was different. It was confident, almost playful. Flynn had a deeper voice, but had always spoken softly, like every word was a secret. Toni asked me once why he always had to be so "mumbly" that she could barely understand him. But I understood him.

Or I thought I had.

"You know what would make this even more fun?" Evan said it loud, as if to the group, but his eyes were only on me.

"What?" I answered.

The side of his mouth lifted up. "If we had a friendly wager."

"Like strip mini golf?" Reece said. "I'm in!"

"Gross," Toni muttered.

I gave Reece a look that said, *Tone it down.* Then I turned back to Evan. "What did you have in mind?"

"A game. To get to know each other better. Like Truth or Dare but only Truth. Whoever wins the hole gets to ask a person in the group one question, and they have to answer."

I gave him a carefree shrug. "You're on."

Toni laughed. "Oh, Evan. You're in trouble. All your secrets are going to come out tonight."

"We'll see," he said, still looking right at me.

"You've underestimated how competitive Morgan is," Toni warned.

"And she's underestimated how good a putter I am."

Reece whistled. "This should be interesting." He led us

through the busted front gate to the first hole. Motioning to Toni, he held his arm out. "Ladies first."

Toni mock curtsied and readied herself at the tee. Bricks surrounded each green. Some cigarette butts and gum mottled the turf, but it was mostly playable. This hole was simple— kidney shaped with a boulder centered on the turf as an obstacle. Someone had spray-painted a penis on the rock.

"I like the graffiti," I said. "It adds to the ambience."

"Classes the place up," Evan agreed.

Toni scowled. "Quiet on the green. I need to concentrate so I can win this hole and ask the first question." Then she winked at me and completely blew the shot. It ricocheted off the boulder and bounced onto the next green.

She smiled. "Whoops!"

That's my Toni, I thought. Master of subtlety.

A few more whoopsies later, she finally maxed out at six strokes and gave up. Reece motioned for me to go, being the next lady and all. I crafted a strategy to aim at the bricks to the right of the boulder, hoping the ball would bounce past it and into the hole. I glanced up. Evan was watching me carefully, as if studying my putting strategy would answer whatever question he had in his head.

I took a deep breath, lined up the putt, and went for it. It hit the bricks where I wanted and missed the hole by an inch. But I tapped it in for an easy two.

Reece went next and also scored a two. I chewed my lip.

If only he'd gotten a three, then I'd be in the clear lead. Evan would probably get a three or a two himself.

"What happens in the event of a tie?" Reece asked.

"We skip a round," Evan answered, not looking up from his club. "Though that won't be necessary."

With a metallic click, his putter gently hit the ball. I thought it was too soft at first, but then it ricocheted off the bricks right where mine had . . . and rolled into the hole.

Evan smiled. "I win."

I had to admit, that smile was pretty sexy. And infectious. Every time he flashed it, I had to smile back, like my body had an involuntary response.

"So who are you going to ask?" Reece said, adding under his breath, "Obvious."

Evan gripped the handle of his putter with both hands. "Morgan."

I stiffened. "Go ahead."

He barely even paused. "Had you ever seen me before the night of Reece's party?"

CHAPTER 11

I didn't know what I'd been expecting, but that question wasn't it. It was interesting, though, and I didn't know how to respond. I had seen Evan online, yeah, but that didn't count. He meant in person.

"No," I answered. "Why do you ask?"

He made a tsk-tsk gesture with his finger. "You don't get to ask a question until you win a hole."

I groaned playfully at his rules, but inside my mind was racing. He wouldn't have asked that unless he thought there was a chance I *had* seen him before. Why would he think that?

"Next hole!" Toni called, racing ahead of us.

On this one, we had to launch the ball up a metal slide and through a clown's mouth. Clowns are creepy in general, but this one was even more so, because it was (a) giant, (b) made of paint-chipped plastic, and (c) missing an eyeball. Toni took three tries to get up the clown's tongue/slide, then two more to get in the hole. I was starting to wonder how much of it was an act to help me win and how much she just sucked at mini golf.

I lined up at the tee, took a couple of practice swings, then hit. I knew right away it was a good putt—not too much power, just enough. It went through the clown's mouth and right into the hole.

I spun around to face Evan. "What do they call that? Oh yeah, a hole-in-one."

He smirked. "Too bad this will be a tie."

"Don't count on it," I replied in a singsong tone.

Reece scored a two, staying consistent.

Evan went next. He took off his jacket and tossed it onto a bench. Underneath he was wearing a plain black T-shirt. As he lined up his shot, my eyes traveled up his forearms and biceps, to the broad shoulder muscles stretching along his back. Reece had mentioned that Evan was a "power hitter" in baseball. It was easy to imagine how good those muscles looked with the shirt *off*.

Evan glanced at me over his shoulder, as if he could feel my eyes burning into him. I blushed and looked away. Lovely. He'd caught me virtually undressing him. That's not embarrassing at all.

Evan hit the ball and I forced myself to focus, readying for the plunk as it dropped into the hole. But the telltale sound didn't come. He sighed and ran his hand through his hair.

Had I . . . *rattled* him?

He needed two more putts to get it in.

"How many was that, Evan?" I joked. "I lost count."

He folded his arms across his chest. "Ask your question."

I decided to fire back the same one. "Had you ever seen *me* before the party at Reece's?"

Evan blinked quickly, showing a slight slip in his confident composure. "In person?" he asked.

I nodded, surprised that he had the same thought process I'd had.

"No," he said.

He seemed honest in his answer, but also taken aback by my question. And now it was my turn to wonder. With his "in person" clarification, he'd obviously seen me somewhere.

"Come on, you guys," Reece called from the next hole.

Toni had already finished by the time Evan and I caught up.

"I got a three!" she called.

This hole had a windmill, and you had to get your ball in the door and through the base of the structure. When the course had been open, the windmill was motorized and the blades spun, adding an extra challenge. I'd always been great at this hole. I was patient and had good timing. But now only two of the three blades remained and they didn't move, taking the challenge away.

"Why don't I start going second," Reece suggested. "Since you guys seem to have this *thing* going on."

That would also conveniently give Reece more time to hang out with Toni at the other end of each hole while they waited for Evan and me to finish.

Toni didn't seem too perturbed by the suggestion, so I said, "Sure. Maybe I can intimidate Evan more playing back-to-back."

Evan laughed from behind me. "You can try . . ."

I kicked at a loose brick while I waited for Reece to finish. I didn't pay attention to his score, but I doubted *he* was even paying attention. Reece and Toni had seemed to accept that this truth wager was just between Evan and me now.

Reece finished and sauntered over to the other side. Toni swept her hair to the side and flashed him a huge smile. I was glad she was being nice like I'd asked. And Reece had used my tips. He wore jeans and a long-sleeve button-down shirt. No overpowering cologne, no gaudy sunglasses. His hair even looked better—lightly tousled instead of hard and spiky. He whispered something in her ear and she laughed. Not her fake laugh, either, because I knew the difference.

Now if only I could figure out why Evan looked at me like I was a big mystery, the night would be a complete success.

I was about to line up my shot when Evan walked to the middle of the green. "What are you trying to do," I said, "distract me?"

"Could I?" he asked with a flirty smile.

I really wished he hadn't caught me checking him out.

"I'm just thinking we should keep it traditional." He reached out and spun the blades of the windmill manually. "Unless you're afraid of a little challenge."

I hid my grin. "Go for it."

Evan kept the blades spinning and I watched them, mentally calculating the distance and speed, waiting patiently for my chance. When I had it, I gave the ball a moderate hit with the club. It went straight, right between the blades and through the open door.

Evan jumped around the windmill to watch it come out the other side. It landed a foot away from the hole. I tapped it in for a two.

"Not bad," Evan said.

I smiled wickedly. "Your turn."

Evan stood at the tee and waited for me to start spinning the blades. I wouldn't cheat. I'd keep the speed steady and consistent. But to reach the windmill without standing on the green itself, I had to tilt way over. I planted my feet on the bricks and leaned forward. My shirt rose slightly as I spun the blades. I felt a kiss of cold air as an inch of skin was exposed to the air.

Evan's eyes were on me.

He putted and the ball bounced off a blade, knocking it into the corner of the green. He muttered a curse under his breath, and I snickered. It took him three more putts to get it in. His worst score yet.

I strolled up to him. "I believe this one's mine."

He inhaled deeply. "Go for it."

"Why did you want to see me tonight?"

"Can't a guy want to be set up with a pretty girl?" That dimple formed again.

Flattery wouldn't sway me. I looked straight at him. "The *real* reason."

He met my gaze, his eyes searching mine for something. He hesitated, far too long for his answer to be honest. "You intrigue me."

We stared at each other for several heartbeats. "How so?" I asked.

He held two fingers up. "That's two questions."

"This one's awesome, guys! Come on!" Toni was bouncing up and down at the next tee.

I wasn't satisfied with Evan's answer, but he walked off and joined Toni and Reece. I'd have to win another hole and figure out a different approach with a new question.

The next hole had been my favorite before this place closed. It opened with a drawbridge over a water hazard. The small pond used to be the brightest color of blue. I'd thought it was magic until my parents explained that it was just dye. In any case, that beautiful crystal water was now green and thick with algae. Over the drawbridge was a big plastic castle. When you walked inside, it was like you were in a cave. It had felt so cool and refreshing on those hot summer days. Now there was probably a family of rodents living inside. I wasn't planning to linger.

Toni shot first and did horribly, as usual. Reece went next, then joined her in the castle. Toni's giggle echoed from the darkness.

"Am I clear to shoot?" I yelled. I didn't need my hole-in-one ruined when the ball bounced off one of them.

Their shadows moved out of the castle and onto the cracked sidewalk behind it. "The green is clear, Miss Serious Golfer!" Toni yelled back.

Then Reece swore, and I heard muttered sighs of disappointment.

"What's going on?" Evan shouted.

"The lower half of the course is flooded!" Reece said. "This is the last playable hole!"

Damn it. I had to win this one. I needed more answers.

Evan stepped closer. "No pressure," he whispered over my shoulder.

I closed my eyes and breathed deeply through my nose. I wouldn't let him get to me. I focused, lifted the club just a tad, and swung. It was a good, strong hit. The ball had no problem getting over the drawbridge and into the castle.

Evan held his arm out. "Let's see where you ended up."

We walked over the bridge and peeked into the castle. My ball was against the wall, in a very bad position.

"Oh, that's too bad," Evan teased. "You can move it away from the wall one club-head length."

"Thanks, Rules Man," I mocked, though I knew the rule, too. I'd played here enough. I placed the ball out, but my shot was still tough. I hit it, hoping for a miracle, and didn't get one. Another putt got the ball in, giving me a total of three. The best I could hope for was a tie.

Evan grinned, resting the club on his shoulder. "My turn."

My jaw clenched. I followed him out of the castle and stood on the bricks lining the drawbridge. His first putt got him over the bridge easily. I squinted into the darkness of the castle. He was stuck in the same position I'd been, against the wall.

"Good luck," I said mockingly.

"Don't need it," he said back.

On the surface he looked just like Flynn, but the more I watched him, the more I saw the differences. Whereas Flynn was skittish and wary, Evan had an easy way about him. Flynn's look was a bit wild and unkempt, and Evan's was cleaned up and controlled. But I had to admit, Evan was hot. The kind of hot that made you feel light-headed and happy and maybe a tiny bit scared. Like cresting the first hill on a roller coaster.

He placed the ball one club-head length away from the wall, lined up his shot, and took it. I closed my eyes, hoping for a miss. But the telltale sound told me it had gone in. He won.

I opened my eyes to Evan standing right in front of me.

"Why did you shine the flashlight in my face at the party?" he asked.

"I wanted to see who you were." *If you were my dead ex-boyfriend.*

Evan raised his eyebrows. "And was I who you were expecting?"

I held up two fingers. "That's two questions."

With a laugh, he returned to the hole and grabbed both of the golf balls. He came back to the bridge and handed mine to me, his finger grazing the skin on my hand, sending a tingling charge throughout my entire body.

I stepped back, almost involuntarily, forgetting that I was on the narrow bridge above the pond. Remembering in mid-step, I tried to regain my footing. But the bricks were slick and my foot slipped. I stuck my arms out for balance, but it was too late. I was falling backward. My eyes widened. I opened my mouth to scream.

Evan threw himself forward and grabbed my arms, in an automatic response. He pulled me toward him, roughly, and I landed face-first against his chest. My senses were all on overdrive from the shock of nearly falling. And now they were overwhelmed with *him*. I could hear his heart beating. His chest rose as he took a deep, relieved breath.

"Sorry," he said, releasing me. "I hope I didn't grab you too hard."

I slowly pulled back. My pulse raced as I looked into his eyes, Flynn's eyes. But then he smiled and Flynn was gone again, though my heart kept racing. I looked over my shoulder at the gross muck I nearly fell into. It was probably only four feet deep. I wouldn't have drowned, but I could've easily come out diseased.

Evan smirked proudly. "I saved you from a messy, algae-related end."

Finally finding my voice, I put my hand over my heart and said, "My hero."

Toni ran over. "Are you okay? I saw you nearly fall in!"

I stepped away from Evan and walked off the little bridge. "Yeah, I'm fine."

"Gotta love those fast baseball reflexes," Reece said. Then he launched into a story about how he was playing first base and caught a foul line drive that would've "killed" the kid sitting on the bench if he'd missed it. I thought it was a tad overdramatic, but he was clearly trying any angle to win Toni over.

We walked slowly back to our cars and I wondered what would happen now. Would we go to dinner? It felt too soon to end the night. I wanted to spend more time with Evan, find out more about him. He strode beside me silently. I wished I could hear what he was thinking.

He touched my elbow, stopping me. "Hey . . ." He spoke softly, like this was a conversation only for me.

I let Reece and Toni walk ahead a few steps, putting some distance between us.

"What?" I asked.

Now that the night was coming to an end, Evan's eyes were

less playful and more determined. He licked his lips nervously. "Do you . . . trust me?"

Our eyes locked. *Yes,* I thought immediately, though I didn't know why. I barely knew this guy and he obviously had his share of secrets. "Why?" I said instead.

"Because, after tonight, I feel like I can trust you. But I'm not sure."

"Trust me with what?" I asked. We obviously *both* had secrets. That's why we were playing that game tonight, warily dancing around each other's words.

He scratched the back of his neck. "If I show you my cards, will you show me yours?"

The game continues . . .

"I'll put them on the table," I said. "But you first."

"Fine," he agreed. "Let's meet tomorrow. Just the two of us." His eyes darkened. "I have something you need to see."

CHAPTER 12

CHAPTER 12

CHAPTER 12

CHAPTER 12

CHAPTER 12

I told Evan I would meet him back at the mini-golf course at noon, so I got there early to take some pictures. Last night had been interesting to say the least. I'd been shocked enough that Evan had wanted to go out with me. But it turned out that *he* was the one who wanted to figure *me* out. I couldn't stop wondering what he had to show me.

I pulled my camera out of its bag at the first green. I laughed again at the interesting choice of graffiti on the boulder and zoomed in. *Click.* That creepy clown was a must-shoot, so I went to that hole next. I took a wide shot and a midshot, but that face was begging for a low angle close-up. I knelt on the green turf and checked the display. Not good enough. If I were a bit lower, the open mouth would seem even more menacing. I lay flat on my belly. My shirt would probably be nasty after this, but the photo was worth it. Propping myself on my elbows, I framed and took the shot. *Click.* Perfect.

That would be one of my favorites, I already knew it. I got up and dusted myself off, then walked to the castle. I knew yesterday that I had to have a photo of this. Once the glorious (by mini-golf standards) highlight of the course, it was now peeling and sad, surrounded by a moat of algae instead of magical blue water.

I focused, then pulled the zoom back to fit the entire castle in the frame. *Click.* I wondered what kind of shot I could get of the inside with this light. I walked up the drawbridge and paused, remembering a moment from yesterday. Before I nearly fell in the water like an idiot. In that brief instant, after Evan touched my hand, I'd felt sparks. It sounded cliché, but there it was. Sparks. Anytime we spoke during the whole date, the air seemed to crackle between us.

With a guilty lump in my throat, I pushed those thoughts away. Toni had spent the rest of last night trying to convince me that I should not only move on, but move on with Evan. As much as she'd hated Flynn, she immediately liked his "non-evil twin" as she called him. But I couldn't go there. Flynn had been dead only three months. I should've still been in mourning, not swooning over someone new.

"Trying to fall again?" a voice called out. "Be careful, because I might not make it in time to rescue you."

I straightened and looked over my shoulder to see Evan standing fifty feet away, wearing the same jeans and black fleece as the night before. And the same sexy grin.

I held up my camera. "Just taking some photos."

He moved closer, interested. "Cool hobby."

"Yeah. And job. I take pictures for the local newspaper sometimes. But this"—I motioned to the rotting golf course—"is for my personal collection."

His eyes narrowed slightly. "You ever do self-portraits?"

Strange question. "No. Why?"

He stuffed his hands into his pockets and shrugged. "Just asking."

The silence stretched on for an awkward moment. "So," I said. "You had something to show me?"

He scanned the area and pointed at the only bench not covered in gum or dried bird poop. "Want to sit down?"

For the first time I noticed the messenger bag slung over his shoulder. "Sure." I followed him to the bench and sat, shivering at the sudden chill in the air.

"This place is kind of creepy, don't you think?" he asked.

I let my eyes roam. Sure, it was empty, run-down, and almost eerily quiet. I could see why Evan thought it had a spooky ghost town feel. But I remembered what it had been like before. I could almost hear kids laughing and families roaring applause for a hole-in-one. For me . . . places like this weren't scary. They were lonely. Yearning for the people to come back.

I couldn't coherently put those thoughts into words for him, though, and I didn't want him to think I was a head case. So I shrugged and said, "I don't mind it."

He turned toward me and our legs touched. I jerked my

knee away instinctively, then felt bad as a hurt look crossed his face. But it wasn't that I didn't find him attractive. I did. I felt something, in that momentary touch. But that's why I pulled away. My brain was too frazzled to play a game of flirty knees right now. I wanted to find out what he knew.

"Down to business," he said, opening the messenger bag.

I tensed, from my shoulders to my toes. This was it. His big secret. A feeling came over me, like whatever was in that bag was going to change everything.

He pulled out a large, thin mailing envelope. "I got this in the mail a little over three months ago. It was addressed to me. I assumed it was another college catalog and let it sit on my desk for a couple of days."

He handed the envelope to me. I eyed it nervously before sliding my finger under the opening and reaching inside. There was only one item. I knew what it was immediately and only by touch. A photograph. I slid it out and my mind exploded.

It was a photo of me.

From the rosebush in the background, I knew I was in my driveway, probably walking from my car to the front door. The foreground was a close-up of my face and shoulders. My features were passive, completely clueless that someone was hiding with a camera, taking my picture.

My voice came out raspy. "Why would someone send you a picture of me?"

"It gets weirder. Flip it over," Evan said dryly.

On the back were words, written in marker in all caps:

IF YOU EVER SEE THIS GIRL—RUN.
DON'T TALK TO HER.
DON'T LOOK AT HER.
JUST LEAVE AND FORGET HER.
LIKE YOUR LIFE DEPENDS ON IT.

Something in my chest twisted. I stared at the words, breathing in and out, trying to make sense of them. My eyes went to Evan, who was watching me warily, like I was about to whip out a knife and stab him because he knew my evil truth. But I had no idea what this meant. None at all.

He looked at me sharply. "Who *are* you?"

My heart pounded wildly. I shook my head. "I'm Morgan. I'm no one."

He eyed me doubtfully.

"Who took this?" I asked.

"I don't know."

"Who sent it?"

"I don't know!" he snapped, sounding almost as scared as I was. "I was hoping *you'd* have some answers for *me*."

I read the words again. "Evan, I don't know what this could mean at all."

"Why would someone go through all this effort to warn me about you?"

"I have no idea." And it was the truth, but I could see now why he'd been so suspicious of me. All of his behavior made sense. Why he was unnerved at the sight of me at the party. And why he'd wanted to see me again. It wasn't that he'd found himself drawn *to* me. He was only trying to find out more information to protect himself *from* me.

"If you have no idea what this means, then why did you show up at a party that I was randomly invited to and shine a flashlight in my face? You want to tell me that's a coincidence?" The distrust in his voice was obvious.

I shifted uncomfortably on the bench. "The party . . . that was something different."

"You knew I was going to be there," he accused. "You knew me."

I averted my eyes. "Kind of."

He pulled the picture out of my hand and stared at it. He was losing his patience. "You'd better give me some answers, Morgan. I think I deserve them."

He was right. It was time to drop the pretense before he became convinced I was a psycho killer. I took a deep breath. "Have you ever heard of a guy named Flynn Parkman?"

He shook his head.

"Well, he was my boyfriend."

Something flashed in his eyes—jealousy?—too quickly for me to recognize it. "So?"

I licked my lips nervously. "He looked exactly like you. Not a little bit. Like, a lot."

Unimpressed, Evan said, "I don't understand what this has to do with anything."

I took a deep breath. "Flynn died three months ago in a hit-and-run accident. I've been . . . dealing with that. A week ago Toni made me upload a photo of him to FriendShare and write some cheesy line. Like a closure thing. Flynn wasn't on Friend-Share, but their facial recognition app suggested I tag the picture with *your* name."

He studied me as I spoke. "A mistake," he said. "I'm sure it happens all the time."

"Yeah, except when I clicked on your name and saw your picture . . ."

He finally caught on. "You thought I really might have been him? What, that he faked his death or something?"

"I didn't really know what was going on. I just needed to know for sure. Toni noticed you were mutual friends with Reece. We got him to invite you to the party so I could see you in person."

"And that's why you ambushed me with the light."

I nodded numbly. "Yeah. And I would've been honest with you sooner, but you acted all cagey and afraid of me."

He looked back down at the picture. "So you honestly don't know why I got this in the mail?"

"No. And it's creeping me out."

He lapsed into silence for a long minute, like he was processing things. Then he met my eyes. "Were you disappointed that I wasn't him?"

"To be honest," I said, "I don't know." I let my mind return to that moment and how I'd felt. "If you had been him, that would've meant my relationship with Flynn was based on lies and betrayal."

"But the alternative . . . that I wasn't him . . ."

"Means he really is dead," I finished.

He spoke quietly. "I'm sorry."

"It's okay. I'd only known and dated him for about two months."

"But still."

I nodded. "It sucks. I think people by nature always want to find closure. And I was almost there . . . until I saw your picture."

He shook his head in disbelief. "How alike could we really look?"

I remembered that the only photo I had of Flynn was also stored on my phone. I pulled it out of my pocket, scrolled to the photo, and held it up. "Look for yourself."

As his eyes settled onto the picture, he immediately flinched.

He took the phone out of my hands. As he brought it closer, his eyes widened.

A heavy feeling settled into my stomach, watching him go through the same emotions I had when I'd seen *his* photo on FriendShare. First shock, then confusion.

"How is this possible?" he asked, his voice shaking.

It was strange that I was the calm one now. I'd had more than a week to wonder about this. "It sounds crazy, but is it possible that you have a twin you didn't know about? Were you adopted?"

He looked up at me with a dazed expression. "No. I have a younger sister, but that's it. I wasn't adopted. My father is a twin, but his brother's dead and he never had any kids of his own."

"But that means twins are in your bloodline."

He rubbed his forehead. "Doesn't it skip a generation or something?"

"Not always, I don't think."

He shook his head. "It's just not possible that I'm a twin. Why would they separate us? It makes no sense."

"Well, now that I've met you in person, I can tell that you're not identical." I pointed at his cheek, though there didn't seem to be a chance of him smiling anytime soon. "Flynn didn't have a dimple. And his hair was black, not brown. Is it possible that you have a brother around the same age?"

"No. No, this is just crazy."

Feeling the urge to comfort him, I gently reached out for his hand. "I'm sorry. I know this has to be overwhelming."

He looked up sharply, like he'd just remembered something.

"What?" I asked.

"Nothing, it's just . . . a nosy neighbor mentioned a few months ago that she saw me prowling around my own yard, peeking into windows. I knew for a fact I hadn't been home at that time. I had practice after school. So I told my parents she was a crazy old bat who was seeing things. But what if . . . what if she saw this Flynn guy?"

That made no sense. "Why would he be creeping around your yard?"

"Why would I look exactly like him? I don't know. All I have right now are questions."

I gazed around at the empty course, like the answers were hidden somewhere in the graffiti or the rot.

Evan lifted the photo. "Is this your boyfriend's handwriting?"

I gazed down at it and shrugged. "I don't know."

"What, he didn't write you love letters?" His voice seemed more jealous than teasing, and I wondered why.

"We texted." I pointed at the words. "But if he *had* written me love letters, I don't think he would have written them in menacing all- caps."

He smirked. "Touché."

I didn't know where to go from here. Every time I got an answer, it created another question. I rubbed my arms. The chill in the air felt like it had seeped into my bones.

"Tell me about him," Evan said suddenly.

I thought for a moment. "He was quiet. Thoughtful. Smart." I paused. "Handsome."

The side of Evan's mouth lifted a bit.

I twisted my hands in my lap. "He was new here and didn't have friends that I knew of, but he enjoyed spending time with me. I think. I actually don't know as much as I thought I did."

Evan's brow furrowed. "What do you mean? He was your boyfriend."

"But he was . . . private. He didn't like to talk much about himself. He said his family was messed up. I accepted that and never prodded."

"But . . . ," Evan said, sensing there was more.

I shrugged. "But then I found out he'd lied about a lot of things. He wasn't enrolled in the private school he claimed he went to. He didn't live at the address he said he lived at. There's actually no record of his family living in town at all."

Evan shook his head. "Well, if he's dead, there has to be a death record or something, right?"

I shrugged. "He only lived here two months. I think his parents probably brought his body back to New Hampshire, where they were from. There wasn't even a funeral or anything here."

"But if he died here, the hospital or someone would have

records, right? I'm just guessing—I don't know how those things work."

I hadn't thought of that. But I *did* know someone who knew how those things worked. Maybe I could get the truth, once and for all.

I grabbed my camera bag and stood up, dusting off my jeans. "I'm going to look into that." I hesitated, not really knowing how to end things. "Thanks for . . . showing me the picture." I knew it had taken a certain amount of trust for him to do that, and I appreciated it.

Evan stood, too, and looked at me, his gray eyes intense. "I don't want this to be the end."

My neck flushed hot. "What?"

"This obviously involves me, too. *I* got the picture in the mail. The guy looks exactly like me."

Oh. The mystery of Flynn. That's what he wanted to be a part of. "Give me your number. I'll let you know what I find out from the death certificate."

"Do you want to meet here again or—"

"I'll call you," I interrupted. I wasn't sure that I wanted to keep meeting him like this. I didn't want to get too close.

Though part of me wondered if I already had.

CHAPTER 13
CHAPTER 13
CHAPTER 13
CHAPTER 13

CHAPTER 13

Cooper didn't work at the Town Hall again until Monday afternoon. I lured Toni to my car with the promise of a ride home and a small detour.

"So what's the detour?" she asked, tossing her bag into the backseat.

"Town Hall. I need another favor from your brother."

"Blergh." She rolled her eyes. "I see enough of that guy at home."

I turned the keys and the engine roared to life. "You'll miss him when he leaves for college in the fall. Admit it."

"Maybe a little." She pointed a finger at me. "But if you ever tell him I said that, I'll text-blast the shaving cream picture of you from the fifth-grade sleepover to everyone we know."

"That'll only get me pity. My best friend accosted me in my sleep and kept photographic evidence. What a monster she is."

Toni laughed. I followed the line of cars out of the school parking lot. When we made it to the road, she said, "Speaking of pictures, did you have any brainstorms over who would send something like that to Evan?"

Toni and I had spent Sunday together at my house, doing homework and watching a movie, and I'd filled her in on everything from my meeting with Evan.

"No," I said. "It doesn't make any sense. Why would I be a danger to anyone?"

I realized too late that the light had turned red, and slammed on my brakes. My worn tires squealed in protest.

"Your driving is a danger to everyone," Toni said.

I gave her a look. "You're distracting me."

"Okay, I won't ask you any more thought-provoking questions for the rest of the drive." She mimicked zipping her mouth closed.

But as I was watching her, the light turned green. The car behind me beeped its horn.

Toni's mouth zipper busted open with a loud laugh.

Minutes later, we walked into the Town Hall and found Cooper sitting at the front desk. At the sight of us, he stood and grinned. "Two dog licenses it is! That will be fifty bucks."

He held his hand out and Toni slapped it, hard. "Ha ha. Very funny."

Cooper looked at me. "Morgan, you know I'm kidding, right?"

Their little sibling squabbles usually entertained me, but

I didn't have the patience for it right then. "I need your help again," I said, getting right to the point.

Toni put her hands on her hips. "And now you *have* to help since you called us dogs."

Cooper held his hands up in defeat. "I am at your service."

I took a deep breath. "Can anyone see a death certificate?"

Cooper raised an eyebrow. "Yeah, sure. Death certificates are considered public-domain documents."

"Can I see Flynn's?"

"We wouldn't have it here. He didn't live here, remember?"

"Would it be filed in New Hampshire, where he was from?"

"First off, you don't even know if that New Hampshire back-story he told you was true. But, no, death certificates are always filed in the state where the person died. He died at the Littlefield Medical Center, right?"

"Yes," I said, remembering the feeling of his heart beating beneath my hand as they placed him on a gurney and put him in the ambulance.

"Then it would be filed in Littlefield."

Evan's town. I nodded. "Okay, I'll go there."

"Wait," he said. "Let me make a quick phone call. I'll meet you guys out front."

I shared a look with Toni, but trusted Cooper enough to do what he said. We walked back outside where I'd parallel parked my car. Toni leaned against the hood and crossed her arms while I paced the sidewalk.

"I'm going out with Reece again next weekend," she blurted out.

I gaped at her. "What?"

She shrugged and a playful little grin lit up her face. "You were right. He's not that bad."

"'Not that bad' isn't a great reason to date a guy."

"Okay, he's more than that. In school he's always been a giant toolface. But it's an act. It's like he pretends to be this character that he thinks everyone will like. But underneath, he's actually really sweet and nice. And, one-on-one, I really like him."

"Yeah, but what are you going to do? Date him on the weekends and hate him during the week when he's Too Cool Reece?"

"I think he's dropping the act. He was my Reece in school today."

"*Your* Reece?" This made me a little worried. Toni didn't fall often, but when she did, it was a twenty-story drop.

"Okay, not *my* Reece. Regular Reece." She beamed. "I think I bring out the best in him."

I reminded myself not to form an opinion too quickly. After all, I was the one who'd told her to take it easy on him. I just didn't realize that to her that meant ending up crazy for him after one weekend.

"Well, I'm happy for you, then."

She smiled. "Thanks."

The door of the Town Hall opened and Cooper strode over to us.

"Don't waste your time," he called.

I blinked. Had he somehow already gotten his hands on the certificate? No. His expression didn't exactly make me feel like good news was on its way.

He shoved his hands into the back pockets of his jeans. "I suspected this, since everything else he told you was a lie. But I didn't want to say anything until I could be sure."

The jagged edge of the car keys bit into my palm as I closed my fist. "What is it?"

"I called the Littlefield Town Hall and asked them to look up the death certificate for Flynn Parkman. They don't have one."

"I thought you said they would have to because he died in their town."

"That's the law, yeah."

"So what does this mean?" Toni asked.

Cooper met my gaze. "It can be only one of two things. Either your boyfriend's name wasn't Flynn Parkman . . . or he's not dead."

CHAPTER 14

I brought Toni home and collapsed on the couch in my empty house. Nothing was what it seemed. Flynn had done nothing but lie to me, maybe even about his own name. And who'd sent a picture of me to Evan?

A dark, awful thought wriggled into my brain like a parasite. What if *no one* had sent that photo? What if Evan took it himself and wrote the warning to get me to trust him? It was a nutball theory, but it wasn't crazier than anything else that was going on.

My cell rang. I gazed down at the number. Speak of the devil.

I held the phone in my hand, suddenly unsure. My finger hovered over the answer button. I let it ring two more times, then, in one jerky motion, hit the green button and put the phone to my ear.

"Hey, Evan."

"Um, hey." He sounded nervous. Not in a suspicious way. More like that adorable "boy on the phone" way. I forced myself to focus.

"I was just calling to see if you'd gotten anywhere with the, um, death-certificate thing. But if you're busy, I can call you back. Or you can call me when you're—"

"It was a bust," I cut in. I told him what we'd found out, and the two choices I was left with. Flynn was never Flynn . . . or he was still alive.

"So what are you going to do now?" he asked.

"I don't know what I *can* do. I can't just walk into the hospital and start asking questions. They have all those patient privacy rules."

"What about the cops?" he said. "River's End is where the hit-and-run happened, right? The police would have details, because they investigated it."

"Yeah, but . . . can I just walk into a police station and start asking questions?" It was probably more public than private info, but this wasn't like bothering Cooper at his after-school job.

"We're in this together, right?" Evan asked.

That awful thought popped up again. That Evan might not have been telling me the whole truth. But what other choice did I have?

"Yeah," I said. "Of course."

"Then let me pick you up after school tomorrow. I have an idea that might get us some answers."

• • •

Evan said he was coming to my house right after school. I knew we got out at the same time, but he had to come from Little-field. So I had time to drop Toni off first, ignoring her repeated requests to come with us, and then ignoring her accusations that I wanted to go alone with Evan not because it was simpler, but because I wanted to "mack out on his face" in the car.

Now I sat on my front steps, left leg bouncing up and down. I wondered if maybe I should wait inside. If sitting on the steps made me look too desperate. But it wasn't a date. I shouldn't have cared how anxious I looked. Before I could change my mind, his gray sedan turned the corner and slid into my drive-way, sunlight glinting off the windshield. Right on time.

I got in the passenger side. The car smelled nice, clean. I clicked the seat belt into place, feeling Evan's eyes on me every second. I glanced over, and it was the first time I saw him and didn't have a rush of Flynn memories. He was completely Evan to me now. A separate person, despite the looks.

"Ready to go?" he asked with a grin. And there was that feel-ing again. His smile kick-started a butterfly convention in my stomach.

"As soon as you tell me where we're going," I said, trying to keep my voice even.

He carefully backed out of my driveway and turned onto the road. "The River's End Police Department."

"We're just going to march in and start asking questions?"

"Nope. I told you I could help. I know somebody there. Or, rather, my family does. We can ask him anything. He won't mind."

I nervously ran my hand up and down the seat belt. I wasn't completely comfortable with the idea, but whatever got us answers. "Okay, let's do it."

Minutes later we were downtown, parked, and walking into the station. The building was small and quiet, not like those loud, busy police stations you see on TV. A receptionist sat behind a heavy glass window.

I hung back as Evan approached her. "Can I speak with Officer Reck, please?"

She barely glanced up. "Your name?"

"Evan Murphy."

The receptionist lifted the phone to her ear, muttered a few quick words into the receiver, and then placed it back down. "He'll be with you in just a moment."

I busied myself by staring at the memos and flyers posted on a bulletin board. There was an out-of-date winter street parking ban, a trash-dumping notice, pedestrian street-crossing safety guidelines, and a sheet with the FBI's top ten most wanted, including thumbnail photos. As if any of them would be in River's End.

The door to the lobby opened, and an intimidating-looking man in police blues entered the room. Evan was tall and athletically built, but this guy dwarfed him. He was the size of an

NFL linebacker. His head was shaved. The lines carved into his face placed him in his midforties. And, at the sight of Evan, he broke into a huge smile. I had the feeling it was something most people didn't get to see.

He gave Evan a pat on the shoulder that probably would've knocked me over. "How's it going, little man?"

"Great!" Evan said. "It's good to see you."

"I probably shouldn't call you little man anymore, though, huh? You're bigger than your dad now, I bet."

"I am."

"Still hitting those balls over the fence?"

"Every game."

"Atta boy." Officer Reck glanced over at me. "Who's the beauty? Your girlfriend?"

Evan blushed. "Um, no, this is—"

"I'm his friend," I cut in.

"That's too bad." He gave Evan a meaningful look. Evan's face turned even redder.

"We're actually here for me," I said, wanting to end Evan's torture. "I was hoping to find out something about a death that happened about three months ago?"

He slid a palm over his giant dome of a head. "What death is that?"

"A hit-and-run on a teenaged boy. On Lincoln Road."

Nodding slowly, he said, "I remember that. Follow me."

He turned and led us down a narrow hallway. Evan and I followed closely. He pointed to a small desk that was strewn with Styrofoam coffee cups and papers. "Have a seat there. Don't mind the mess. Maid's day off."

I sat stiffly in a hard plastic chair while Evan settled into the one beside me. "So he's a family friend?" I whispered.

"Yeah. He and my dad go way back. I thought he could help."

A moment later the cop returned with a file in his hand. He sat down on the other side of the desk, the chair groaning beneath him. He opened the file and read quietly for a moment, I assumed reacquainting himself with the case. Then he snapped the folder shut.

"Okay, what are you here to find out?" he asked.

Only everything, I thought. My throat tightened as I prepared to ask the question.

Evan leaned forward in the chair and asked before I could. "Did the boy die?"

The officer looked from Evan to me and back. "Can I ask why you want to know?"

I exhaled hard. "He was my boyfriend."

"And you don't know if he's dead or alive?" he asked skeptically.

"I thought he was dead . . ." I stopped myself. I didn't want to get into every little detail. "But, long story short, either he's alive or he gave me a fake name."

Officer Reck tapped his fingers against the folder. "What did he say his name was?"

"Flynn Parkman."

He looked at me differently then. With pity, perhaps. He opened his mouth, and before the words came out, I knew what they were. I could feel them slithering around me, tightening across my chest.

"I'm sorry to be the one to break the bad news," he began. "The boy *is* dead. He died at the Littlefield Medical Center. And his name wasn't Flynn Parkman."

A hole opened in my heart. Grief, betrayal, all the emotions I'd felt over the last few days rushed through me. He was dead *and* a liar. Evan kept glancing at me, as if to make sure I was all right. I didn't want to lose it. Not here, not now.

I forced the words out of my throat. "What was his real name?"

The officer glanced down at the file. "James Bergeron."

James, I thought. So classic, so ordinary. It sounded wrong in my mind. But the Flynn in my mind wasn't real. James was real. That's who he was whether I liked it or not.

"Is his family still living in town?" I asked.

Officer Reck shook his head. "He was a runaway."

My head rocked back. I knew his family life had been bad; he'd told me as much. But to run away? "Does his family know that he's dead?"

A dark look crossed the officer's face. Not pity, something worse. "He had no family."

My breath caught. "What?"

"He lived in a foster home in New Hampshire and—for unknown reasons—left and settled somewhere in the area here."

A thousand possibilities ran through my mind. Had he stopped here on his way to somewhere else, met me, and stayed? Was he always planning to move on? Is that why he'd broken up with me? He was ready to go on to the next town and keep running . . .

Or had he chosen River's End on purpose and I was merely a complication? If so, why had he been here?

Officer Reck crossed his meaty hands on top of the desk. "When you and this boy were together, where did he bring you? What was his address?"

I chewed my lip. "Um, he was . . . private. He said his family life was bad. So he only came to my house. I never went to his."

"Where did you meet?"

For some reason, I didn't want to share that. I wanted to keep one thing for myself. And a gut feeling deep down told me to lie. "At Happy Time Mini Golf," I blurted.

I could see Evan looking at me out of the corner of my eye. He was probably wondering why I hadn't mentioned that when we were sitting there on the bench Saturday. I could see the distrust start to creep back into his expression.

I didn't like how this had changed from me asking questions

to me being questioned. I'd gotten what I came for. There was no reason to stick around.

I stood and held out my hand. "Thanks for your help, Officer Reck. I'll let you get back to work now."

He stood slowly, as if reluctant to let me go. He took my hand and shook it, gently, but I still felt like I was facing off against a bear.

I started walking back toward the lobby, not even waiting for Evan. He caught up with me outside, halfway to the car.

"Sorry," he said, slowing his jog to a walk. "I had to say my good-byes."

"No problem. I just wanted to get out of there. I know the truth now." I stopped by the passenger side of his car, but Evan made no move to unlock the door.

He stared at me, through me. "You lied to him about the mini-golf place."

I answered simply. "Yes."

"Why?" He didn't ask where Flynn and I *had* met. He only wanted to know why I'd lied to the cop.

"I don't know, fully," I answered. "I just wanted to keep it to myself. That memory."

"Is it true that James refused to ever bring you to his house?"

I winced at the name. "Can we keep calling him Flynn? James just sounds wrong."

"Whatever you want." He hesitated. "Is it true? He never told you *anything*?"

It made Flynn sound terrible. And, yes, Flynn was broody and negative and all those dark things, but—until that horrible night—he seemed to adore me. He made me feel special. Who doesn't like feeling special? But I couldn't explain that to Evan. It made me feel stupid. Like a dumb girl with a crush who accepted whatever scraps her boyfriend was willing to toss her.

"Yes, it's true," I said softly.

Surprise registered on Evan's face. "And you put up with that?"

"What?"

"Well, it's just that you don't seem like the type to put up with any bull."

I liked that he saw me that way. I tilted my chin up a little higher. "Maybe I was then. Maybe I'm changing."

"Good," he said, nodding. "You deserve to be treated better than that."

I snorted. "Now you sound like Toni."

He raised his eyebrows. "She didn't like him?"

I smirked. "Not at all." But it was clear now that she'd been right not to trust Flynn all along. I should've listened to her.

I gazed up at Evan. He was staring at me with an expression so intense, it made my knees tremble. He wanted to kiss me. I could see it in his eyes, in his slightly parted lips.

But I couldn't give that to him, even after everything he'd done for me today. Instead, I slipped my arms around his neck and gave him a hug. I'd expected Flynn's outdoorsy scent, but Evan smelled like soap and shampoo. Clean and fresh.

The two of them were different in every way.

I pulled back, and the look in his eye was gone.

"Come on," he said. "I'll drive you home."

CHAPTER 15
CHAPTER 15
CHAPTER 15
CHAPTER 15

CHAPTER 15

Back when both my parents worked down the street at Stell, we had family dinner at home five nights a week. Now, that was a rare occasion. Dad usually ate on the train on the way home from the city. Mom shoved a sandwich into her mouth while driving from one job to the next. And I helped myself to whatever I could scrounge in the cabinet. I'd been planning on heating up a can of SpaghettiOs for myself when Evan dropped me off, but my parents were actually both home.

I walked through the front door, expecting the inquisition. *Where were you? Your car was in the driveway. Who were you with?* But as I slid off my shoes and padded toward the kitchen, I heard it again. That insistent whispering.

They thought I was upstairs in my room.

They hadn't even come up to say hi to me.

They were so lost in their own world that they didn't hear my footsteps, didn't notice me until I entered the kitchen.

Dad's eyes widened and he gave a slight shake of his head,

a silent message to Mom that it was time to stop talking about *it*. Whatever *it* was.

I stood in front of the refrigerator, where a crayon drawing I'd made of our family hung beneath a happy-face magnet. I'd made the picture when I was eight, but Mom refused to take it down.

"What's going on?" I asked.

"Just trying to figure out what to make for dinner," Mom said cheerily. But it was fake. Oh so fake.

"Were you fighting?" I posed the question to my dad since Mom was already halfway down Cover-Up Road.

"Of course not," he said, joining her.

Mom made for the fridge, but I didn't budge. "Can you move, honey? I want to see what we have for food."

"Why are you both home?" I asked. "Isn't it early?"

"It's a wonderful coincidence that we both got out early," Mom said. "It's not often we get to have family dinners anymore."

"Yes," Dad piped up. "Let's not look a gift horse in the mouth."

Wonderful. We'd moved on to clichés. Whatever was going on, they weren't about to let me in. Not tonight anyway. I moved aside to let Mom open the fridge. She smiled with her mouth closed.

Mom quickly made spaghetti and we sat around the table,

eating and talking about things that didn't matter. *The weather should be warming up soon. That tree in the backyard is dead; it'll probably have to come down. How is the yearbook photography coming, Morgan?*

I thought about telling them everything. That I had found a boy who looked just like Flynn. That Flynn had lied. That I'd been looking into his past, trying to figure out the truth. But the words stuck in my throat. I didn't want to worry them, to add to their stress. And—I'm not proud of this—a small part of me didn't want to share with them because I was angry that they were keeping secrets from me.

By the time I got up to my room, I had three missed calls from Toni. I crawled on top of my covers, called her back, and filled her in on everything Evan and I had found out.

"Whew." She let out a long breath. "So how are you holding up?"

"I'm fine."

"Hi, Morgan? This is me, Toni, your best friend. The one you actually tell the truth to."

I let out a small laugh.

"So how about you tell me how you're *really* doing?"

I shrugged, though she couldn't see it. "Flynn was already dead, so it's not like I'm grieving all over again."

"But?" she prodded.

"But it hurts that he lied to me about everything. And I don't know why. I don't understand it." I think that was the worst part of it. That I didn't know *why*.

And meanwhile, something was going on with my parents. Something they didn't want to burden me with. I wondered if one of them was losing their job again. If we were at risk of losing the house. My mind sprinted to all the worst-case scenarios. But I couldn't share those worries with Toni, because she was *living* the family drama that I only feared.

"What did you do today?" I asked.

She let out a dreamy sigh and started rattling off every detail of her afternoon with Reece. I was delighted that she was happy, even though I didn't fully trust Reece yet. He still hadn't proved to me that he'd left that whole Too Cool act behind. But as she relayed every "totally cute" thing he said, my mind wandered.

Why had Flynn been in River's End? Did he just pick the town randomly? Could it really be a coincidence that a boy who looked just like him lived a couple of towns over?

I looked back on certain memories differently now, knowing the truth. Like when he told me his name. Had there been any sign it was a lie? Had his eyes flicked around, taking in the surroundings . . . coming up with the last name Parkman because we were standing in a closed amusement park?

"You're not listening to me . . . ," Toni singsonged into the phone.

"Sorry." I groaned. "I'm a bad friend right now. I'm not all here."

"So where are you?"

"Thinking about Flynn, the day we met, when the lies began."

Silence hung between us for a long moment. Toni said quietly, "You still haven't been back there. To Fantasy World."

"Not past Larry the Lion, no. But I want to. I've wanted to take more shots there for a while. I imagine they'll be the crown jewel of my portfolio of abandoned places."

Toni snorted. "Your pictures are creepy and you are some kind of weird, Morgan Tulley. But it's time."

"For what?"

"For you to return to the place where you met Flynn Parkman. Tomorrow after school. I'll be your moral support. Bring your camera."

King's Fantasy World wasn't a big amusement park, even when it had been open. It billed itself as "family amusements," which meant it was for little kids. At around ten years old it became cool to not care about the park anymore, though we all still secretly liked it as we outwardly called it lame. Kids didn't really stop coming until they were teens. But the park closed when I was twelve, so I never had the chance to fully outgrow it.

Having something taken away before you're ready to let go always hurts.

Now, Larry the Lion bared his plastic teeth at Toni and me, warning us not to go past the fence. As easily as River's End teens played at the empty Happy Time Mini Golf, we avoided King's Fantasy World. There were too many darkened corners and hidden dangers.

Toni gazed up at the fence. "Do we just . . . climb it?"

I remembered the last time I'd climbed that fence, the day I met Flynn. I'd nearly hanged myself by my camera strap while scrambling over the top. There had to be an easier way.

"Hold on a sec," I told her. I followed the fence, letting my fingers trail along the chain-links, until I came to a sharp point.

"Oww!" I pulled my hand away.

Toni hurried to my side. "What happened?"

I squeezed my finger where an angry scratch stung my skin. "The links are cut here," I said, realizing what I'd found.

I pulled hard, stretching the edges open as far as they'd go. "Squeeze through," I told Toni.

She slipped inside easily, then held the hole open for me. The metal grazed my arm, fraying an inch of my sweatshirt, but I made it.

We pushed through the high hedges and then stopped for a breath. We were in.

"It's like going back in time," Toni said.

I let my eyes take everything in. I'd spent so many hours here when it was open, running from ride to ride, following the tinny music, begging my parents for fried dough and cotton candy. But it was different now. Trash was strewn about the grounds. Grass, struggling for life, pushed its way up the cracks in the pavement.

The kiddie coaster, the park's only thrill ride, rose between overgrown trees in the distance. I could almost hear the click-clack of the car going up the hill. It seemed so small and unintimidating now. But when I was little, I thought that hill rose halfway to the clouds. I remembered the first time I rode the coaster. It was both exhilarating and completely terrifying at the same time. I thought my little heart was going to burst out of my chest. I screamed through the whole ride. When it ended, my dad turned to me with a worried look on his face and asked, "Are you all right?" Fists in the air, I yelled, "Again!"

Sure, it had been terrifying, but it was a safe scare. I knew I'd be all right in the end.

"Come on, let's walk around," Toni said now.

We started moving forward, slowly. My camera felt heavy around my neck and I lifted it, poised and ready. A patch of moss grew in the shaded area beneath a ticket counter. I brought the camera up to my eye. *Click.* I took a shot of the Ferris wheel looming in the distance. Its bucket cars had been disassembled and sold, so only the spokes and rods were left behind, like a metal skeleton.

A plastic bag skittered past us, billowing in the wind, and I followed until it came to rest against the old refreshment stand, which was almost completely covered in graffiti. On one panel of rotting wood, giant bubble letters declared that Susan loved Chris. I zoomed in to capture it.

"Can we see the carousel?" Toni asked.

"Sure." I vaguely remembered its location, somewhere near here.

"It's behind that kiddie car ride," Toni said, pointing.

The kiddie cars followed a thick metal track. The steering wheels were purely ornamental, but we didn't realize that at the time, being delusional little kids. We thought we were really driving. Now the cars were rusted. One was hanging half off the track. *Click.*

"There it is!" Toni cried, and rushed to the carousel.

I knew why she was so excited. The carousel had been her favorite ride. I remembered there was a pink horse that she always chose. If it was taken, she'd wait for the next ride just so she could sit on that one.

But as we approached the carousel, I couldn't tell which one was her pony. The horses were still and quiet, their paint chipped and faded. The mirror panels were so dirty, I couldn't even see a reflection. Part of me had wished they'd dismantled the ride and sold it off to live in another park somewhere. But it had been left behind to rot, choking in weeds. *Click.*

Toni scowled, her excitement gone. "This place is creepy," she complained. I didn't exactly disagree.

I remembered the day I met Flynn, the last day I'd been here. I was breaking the rules, which was unlike me, but I'd figured it was okay since it was "for my art." We'd all been warned . . . *Bad things happen in the park. Avoid it.* But I'd figured those marauding bands of druggies and criminals only lived in parents' overprotective imaginations. This was still River's End, after all. Not the city. But, just to be safe, that day I'd planned to stay out in the open. I wasn't going to enter any of the buildings or climb onto any of the old rides. Those first few minutes inside the park . . . it had been so quiet. I'd felt completely alone. And I'd realized that was the real reason people avoided the park. Not because of any imaginary hooligans, but because it was—by nature—so damned creepy. The deeper I'd explored, the more frightened I felt.

But then I saw Flynn. And he didn't look the slightest bit nervous. He was leaning against the fun house like he owned it.

"Where to now?" Toni asked, snapping my brain back into focus. She rubbed her arms through her jacket, though it wasn't cold out.

"The fun house," I said. "I need to see it."

We retraced our steps to the graffiti-covered refreshment stand. I knew how to get to the fun house from there. We took a right, past the giant parallel racing slides, where cracks in the plastic carved winding paths that no person would race on again.

And there it was. Standing just as it had that day months ago.

The fun house was painted black and purple, and a giant

evil clown head crowned the top of the doorway. Even though it had been cheesy and full of cheap scares, I'd loved it when I was younger. I remembered the tipsy room, the black-light hallways, the mirror maze. Even at the exit, when you thought you were safe, an air blast at your face combined with a loud horn gave you one last fright.

"It looks the same," Toni said.

A slow smile spread across my face. "I wonder what it's like inside."

Toni's eyes widened. "No way."

I nodded. "Way."

She shook her head quickly. "I won't go."

I did my best chicken imitation, clucking and waving my elbows.

She stuck her chin out. "I'm not going to fall for that."

Usually I was the one trying to talk her out of doing something crazy, not the other way around. "It was your idea to come here, remember? Plus, what are you scared of?"

She counted off on her fingers. "Serial-killing vagrants, rat disease, bat infestations, dead things, ghosts."

"None of those are in there," I assured her.

"How do you know?"

I started walking, dry grass crunching under my shoes. I called out, "I'm going in with or without you. So you can come with me . . . or stay out here *alone*." I stretched the last word out in the creepiest voice I could muster.

"Fine!" Toni stomped up beside me. "Though I'm only coming so I can protect you from whatever horrible terror awaits you in there, because I'm the bestest best friend ever."

I hid my grin. "I appreciate it."

I reached the door that had been the entryway. There was no knob, and planks of wood were nailed across it.

"That's too bad," Toni said, already backing away. "Oh well, we tried!"

I held my hand out. "Slow your roll, chicken. There's another way." I pointed to the side of the building, where the exit had been.

Toni's mouth dropped open. "No, no, no." She sounded like a toddler on her way to a tantrum. "That's where they blow the horn in your face and the air blasts at you."

"You really think that's still working? The electricity was cut to this place years ago."

"What if it didn't run on electricity?"

"Face your fears!" I yelled and started jogging the length of the building.

"Don't leave me here!" Toni said, half laughing, half legitimately scared.

We turned the corner to where the exit had been, and it was still there. Just a black painted door. No planks, no giant bolts. I reached out for the knob, expecting it to be stiff, but it turned.

"It's unlocked," I whispered. Though I didn't know why I suddenly felt the need to lower my voice.

"Fantastic," Toni snarked back.

Once the knob turned completely, the door released and slowly opened inward with an eerie creak. Outside light illuminated the first couple of feet of flooring. But then after that—darkness.

"You are *not* going in," Toni said behind me, her voice panicked.

"I am." That memory of Flynn leaning up against the building had stirred something inside me. I was determined to have a look.

"This is how every teen horror flick starts. You're like the stupid girl you yell at in the movies."

"I'm not the stupid girl. There's nothing in here. It's daytime. And this isn't a horror movie." I tentatively stepped on the square of wood that used to trigger the blast horns. Nothing. That was a relief. The slightest noise would send Toni tearing out of here. She was sticking so closely to my back, I could feel her breathing on my neck.

"I can't see anything," she said, peeking over my shoulder. "Didn't there used to be a window in here?"

This had been the final room to the fun house. Lit by black lights, it had painted monsters on the walls, and a window where kids waiting outside could pop their faces up or bang on the glass to scare their friends. I turned to the right, where I remembered it being. A dim yellow glow came from the area.

"What are you doing?" Toni screeched.

"I'm finding the window." I took slow steps over to the yellowish glow, my hands out in front of me. Finally reaching it, I felt something under my fingertips. I ripped at it, and sunlight poured in.

Toni held her hands up to her eyes and yelled like a vampire being scorched.

"The window was covered with old newspaper," I said. "I just tore it down."

"Warn my retinas next time!" she yelled.

She brought her hands down and both of us waited a beat for our eyes to adjust to the light. The monsters were still painted on the walls—a werewolf, a vampire, a ghost baring sharp teeth. Though they were more cheesy than creepy now. But the room was no longer empty as it had been back in the day.

A thick blue sleeping bag lay unrolled by the far wall. A battery-operated camping lantern lay beside it. A pile of clothes sat folded in the corner, and beside those was a ratty black backpack.

"Someone's living here," Toni whisper-screamed. "You promised! You said no serial-killing vagrants!"

I knelt by the sleeping bag and ran my fingers over the top of the nylon. It was dusty. No one had slept here in a while. I picked the first item of clothing off the top of the pile and unfolded it. It was a thin, black T-shirt with a swirly blue design in the center.

I recognized it.

"This is Flynn's shirt," I said.

Toni paled and her eyes went to the backpack. I grabbed it, yanking the zipper open, and turned it upside down. I wanted all his secrets to spill out onto the floor, but instead it was only toiletries—a comb, a toothbrush, toothpaste, a deodorant stick.

"He was living here," Toni said quietly.

I pushed myself back up to standing and looked at the mess. I couldn't believe it. He was a runaway, sure, but I just assumed he'd been staying with someone.

My chest hurt. I would've helped him somehow, if he'd told me. Why would he stay here?

Toni had picked up the backpack and started squeezing it. "There's something else in here."

She held the bag out to me and I unzipped the front pocket. I reached inside and pulled out a small notebook with a pen stuck in the coil. I flipped through and read a few of the scribbled notes inside. They made no sense to me. There were a few mentions of Stell Pharmaceuticals, which was weird. One page just had the sentence *Cops on the take.*

"This is really messed up," Toni said, practically taking the words right out of my mouth.

I flipped from back to front, skipping all the blank pages, in an effort to find the last thing he wrote. I stopped when I found the final page. This one was different. Instead of a hurried, barely readable script, his handwriting was neater, purposeful. My heart began hammering wildly in my chest as I read the first two words. It was a note, and it was addressed to me.

Dear Morgan,

I'm writing this in case something happens. Don't come looking for me. I want you to move on with your life.

Forget me.

I want you to know that you're the best thing

The note ended abruptly, as if he had been interrupted.

But now I knew. He *had* cared about me. The breakup in the car was just . . . what . . . him thinking he was protecting me? A tear leaked out of the corner of my eye. I didn't wipe it away. I let it trail down my cheek and drop to the dusty floor. I wished he'd gotten to finish the note. I wished he'd been more honest with me.

"Whoa," Toni said, reading the page over my shoulder. "You know what this means, don't you?"

I nodded. "He was interrupted and didn't get to finish the note."

She knocked on my head. "Hello, Morgan! Wake up and smell the conspiracy."

I blinked quickly. "Conspiracy?"

"All his weird notes. Mentioning the cops. Then writing a

good-bye note to you in case something happens. He stumbled onto something. Something big."

I looked at Toni through glassy eyes. "What are you saying? Do you think he was murdered?"

She shrugged. "Think about it."

The night Flynn was killed, my instincts had told me he'd been waiting on that road for someone. He kept looking around and acting nervous. My insecurities had immediately jumped to thoughts of another girl. But now I wondered if someone else had told him to meet there. Someone who could have been involved in this. His strange behavior made more sense. Why he'd wanted me away from there. Why he started a fight when I pushed him for answers.

He was trying to protect me.

Familiar feelings of guilt gnawed at me. If only I could have kept him in the car. If only . . .

CHAPTER 16
CHAPTER 16
CHAPTER 16

CHAPTER 16

I stayed up too late trying to make sense of the chicken scratch in Flynn's notebook. At best, they were barely readable notes. At worst, they looked like the rantings of a madman. There were dates—none of which meant anything to me—and names I could barely decipher. Even some algebra. One page only said $NT=X$. I saw the word *Stell* a couple of times. I assumed he was referring to the company. After a while, many notes included only the initial *S*. Were those also referring to Stell? Why had he been researching the company? And what was up with *Cops on the take*? Flynn was insanely private and a liar, yes. But was he a crazy person, too?

I kept the notebook tucked in my backpack at school Thursday. For some reason I wanted to have it by my side at all times. Like if I kept it at home or in my locker, it would disappear. Maybe just reading Flynn's thoughts was turning me into a paranoid freakazoid like him.

We had a quiz in pre calc, but in my other classes, my mind wandered. I revisited the night of the accident again and again. But now the black SUV was increasing its speed and purposefully swerving toward Flynn. My memory was changing to accommodate the new information. I couldn't even trust my own brain.

The note he left for me wasn't evidence that he was murdered. Yeah, it seemed shifty that he left a note "in case something happens," and something did, in fact, happen. But that might have been a coincidence. I didn't exactly have anything to take to the police. Especially after they had already investigated the hit-and-run. And double especially when the notebook insinuated that the cops themselves were corrupt.

The last bell rang, and I grabbed what I needed from my locker, then wandered over to Toni's to see if she needed a ride home. But she had her back to her locker and her tongue in Reece's mouth.

"Eww, guys," I said. "PDA is so first boyfriend, freshman year."

They—thankfully—separated their faces. Toni giggled and tucked her hair behind her ears. "What's up, Morgan?"

I shifted my backpack to my other shoulder. "Do you want me to drive you home?"

"Nah, I'll give her a ride," Reece said, and made a thrusting motion with his hips as if the joke itself wasn't obvious enough.

Toni gave him a look that could freeze a fireball in midair.

He cast his eyes down like a scolded dog. "Sorry."

She looked back at me. "He's a work-in-progress. But, yeah, he'll drive me home." Then she pointed down the hall. "Oh! I left my notebook in Spanish. Be right back." She shuffled off with a giant goofy grin on her face.

It worried me. I wasn't quite convinced that dating Reece was a good idea. And Toni didn't date lightly. She fell hard. It happened twice freshman year and once in tenth grade. She also tended to forget she had a best friend during these times. Until the relationship crashed and burned and her crying face became a permanent fixture in my bedroom every afternoon. But, if I warned her not to go too fast with Reece, she'd just tell me that this time was different. That's what she said every time.

I felt sort of awkward, momentarily abandoned with Reece. "So . . . how are things in Happy Love Land?"

I expected a Too Cool Reece response since we were in the school hallway and all, but he only smiled and said, "It's great."

I took a moment to take in everything about him. Despite his momentary slip a minute ago, his look, his demeanor, all seemed to be dedouchified. Undouched, if you will. "You're different," I said.

"It's nice not to have to be *on* all the time, you know?"

His sincerity chipped away at my skeptical little heart. "So you really like her?"

"A lot."

Toni being lovestruck wasn't as bad if Reece was equally so. But still, it couldn't hurt to give him one last tip. I took a step closer and lightly pressed my finger into his chest. "Good. Because if you hurt Toni, they will find your body in twenty-seven pieces at the bottom of the river. Got it?"

He smiled and swatted my finger away. "Got it."

Toni returned at that moment, witnessing my threat. She rolled her eyes. "Is Morgan getting all best friend protect-y?"

"Protective," I said.

"You've got nothing to worry about," Reece said, grabbing her hand.

I wanted desperately to believe that this wouldn't end in tears. That this would be different from Austin in ninth grade or Corey in tenth. But the way Reece looked at her, like she was an amazing miracle and he was lucky to just be standing by her side, gave me hope.

And for some reason, it made me think of Evan. Not Flynn, which was weird, so I pushed the thought away.

"Yeah, yeah," I said, shooing them off. "Go have fun playing tonsil hockey."

"I'll call you later!" Toni yelled as she hurried away from me.

I'd barely reached my car when my cell rang. I pulled it out of my bag and put the phone to my ear. "Hello?"

"Morgan, it's Felicia at the paper."

A group of girls walked by practically yelling rather than talking. I got into my car and closed the door so I could hear. "Hi, Felicia. What's up?"

"Want an assignment? You'd have to go right now."

"I can do that," I said.

She let out a sigh of relief. "Great. Rebecca is in labor and Chris is at his other job. You're my only freelancer available."

"Where do you need me?"

"There was a suicide at the falls. A man who'd lost his home to foreclosure, then his wife took the children and left. Yada, yada."

My stomach lurched, but Felicia continued as if she were ordering from a menu. "We'll need a photo of the falls, from whatever angle makes them seem most treacherous. And if anyone has laid a wreath or some sort of memorial there, I want a shot of that, too. Double pay if you get crying mourners. You have the release form for them to sign?"

"Yep," I squeaked. I always had extra release forms in the car. People needed to sign them before you could use their photograph in the paper. But I wouldn't bring one to the falls today. If anyone was there, crying, I wouldn't take a picture of them. It just felt wrong.

"I'll e-mail you what I get," I said.

• • •

Cascade Falls was beautiful, especially after weeks of heavy rain, when the waters raged as if controlled by an angry, invisible hand. During the Great Depression, they'd been dubbed Suicide Falls. Reason: obvious. But jumpers went over only once every couple of years now. Including this morning, apparently.

The falls were in what used to be a River's End town park. But the park lost its funding, the land overgrew, and now it was yet another place in town that once held beauty and now only sadness.

It was usually an empty area. Sometimes you'd find a couple attempting to have a picnic, but they'd try it only once. The falls were loud. And mist sometimes blew in your face when the wind changed direction. So it wasn't as romantic as it looked from a distance.

Today, though, as I parked my car in the lot and walked the well-worn trail to the waterfall, I knew I wouldn't be alone. If I've learned one thing from my newspaper job, it's that tragedy attracts looky-loos. And there they were. Just a handful of people milling around, but they wouldn't have been there on a normal day. They were curious. The type of people who slow down to gaze at the carnage of a car wreck.

I didn't want to stay any longer than I had to. The whole scene felt morbid to me. I got as close to the top as I safely could and snapped a photo looking down. It was probably a fifty-foot drop, dangerous in and of itself, but the river's wild current dragged you down after that. There was no surviving a fall here.

I shivered as the misty spray spat at the nape of my neck below my ponytail. I took another handful of shots, then worked my way down the trail to the bank of the river to take some pictures from below. I was more comfortable there. Away from the dizzying heights. Down where the air was drier, the waterfall's roar less ear-splitting.

I snapped more photos from this position and knew from previewing them in the display that one of these would be the winner. From below, the waterfall seemed even more menacing. For good measure, I took a couple of shots of the river itself. The water was dark, almost black, with a churning white surface.

A makeshift memorial was beginning to grow on the largest rock on the riverbank—a few flowers, a candle. At least the looky-loos paid their respects while they were here. Though, now, as I cast a glance around, I realized most of them had returned to their lives, their curiosity sated. Only one person remained, a man about my dad's age. He wore a business suit and stood facing the waterfall, staring at it with an expression I could almost, but not quite grasp. Regret, maybe?

He probably knew the guy who'd jumped. He would probably stand there all afternoon, wishing he could go back in time and save him.

But I knew there was no going back. No matter how much you tried to relive a moment. How much you wished you could change one small thing, bump the time line, know then what you know now.

Once the dead are gone, they're gone.

CHAPTER 17
CHAPTER 17
CHAPTER 17
CHAPTER 17

CHAPTER 17

The school day dragged on Friday. The highlight was a slice of tastes-like-cardboard pizza from the cafeteria. After the last bell, I stood at my locker and filled my backpack with whatever books I'd need for the weekend. I checked my phone for new messages. Felicia e-mailed that she'd chosen two of my photos—the shot of the falls from below and the one of the makeshift memorial.

Part of me had been hoping for a text or missed call from Evan.

I slipped the phone back into my pocket and tapped my fingernails against the locker door. I could always call *him*. I *did* have information to share. And nothing to do. Toni had plans with Reece.

I felt the weight of my cell phone in my pocket. I wanted to call him. But thinking about him made me nervous, excited, and a bit light-headed, and that scared me. So as I drove home, I talked myself out of calling. I would ignore the ache in my chest that told me I wanted to see him again. It was too soon to feel this way about someone. And too strange that Evan looked so much like Flynn. Everything about the situation was overwhelming.

I would spend my Friday at home, I decided. I could do my homework, get that out of the way. Maybe watch TV with my parents, see if they were acting normal again.

But, you know, a girl plans, and fate laughs right in her face.

When I got to my house, Evan's car was parked on the street out front.

I pulled into the driveway, and he got out of his car, walking slowly, hands in his pockets. I met him halfway across the front yard. Neither of us spoke for a moment. Then I said, "Hi."

He looked up at me with an adorably awkward smile. "I hope you don't mind that I stopped by."

I could feel my cheeks flush. "No, not at all." *I was just obsessively thinking about you, so it's fine.*

"I just . . . I was going to call, but then I found myself driving here instead." He paused and looked at me. Like *really* looked at me. Like he was trying to see inside my mind, inside my soul. "How are you?" he asked.

My throat suddenly felt dry. "Good . . . okay . . . weird."

He raised an eyebrow. "Weird?"

"There have been some developments," I explained.

He aimed a thumb over his shoulder at my house. "Want to go inside and talk?"

I chewed on my lip for a moment. My parents weren't back

from work, but what if he stayed until they got home? "Can we go to your place instead? It's just . . . if my parents come home. I haven't told them about you yet and . . . how much you look like . . . him."

He swallowed hard and hesitated a moment, like he was unsure about something. Then he smiled, that dimple showing again, and said, "Sure. Hop in, I'll drive."

I hefted my bag up onto my shoulder and followed him to his car.

He gave a sideways look to my backpack. "Plan on doing some homework at my house?"

"That development I was talking about is *in* here." I patted the bag.

"Intriguing," he said with a smirk.

We made small talk about school until he turned quiet as we slowed to a stop at the top of his massive driveway in front of his ridiculous house. I realized, at his silence, that he was expecting some sort of reaction. *Oh yeah,* I remembered. He didn't know that I had done some mild stalking with Toni and already knew he lived in a mansion.

I faked the best gasp I could. "Wow. Quite a humble cottage you have here."

"That's kind of why I didn't want to bring you home," he admitted. "I don't want you to . . ."

"Think you're some spoiled rich kid?"

He smiled. "Yeah, for starters."

"It's good that I got to know you first, then."

He still didn't look comfortable. But I didn't care if a person had money or didn't. My family had been comfortably upper middle class, and now we were struggling day by day to hold on to everything we'd earned. But we were still the same family, the same people.

"So . . . are you going to invite me in?" I asked.

His face relaxed. "Yeah, let's go."

I followed him through white double doors and into the foyer. He tossed his keys onto a marble table beneath a gold-framed mirror. In the reflection, I caught the curve of a spectacular staircase. One that you see and immediately picture yourself slowly walking down, wearing some beautiful ball gown. This seemed more like a movie set than a house.

"We can head to the library," Evan said.

A library. Of course he had a library.

I followed him down the hall, my shoes squeaking on the glossy floors. Every inch of the space was immaculate. The only thing that stood out was a window in a den held together with masking tape. I pointed as we passed. "What happened there?"

Evan winced. "That's my bad. I was practicing in the yard with a friend from the team, and a baseball broke the window. My parents are getting a new one today, and then we have to get the alarm company out to rewire the window sometime next week. It's a whole big thing."

I wanted to ask him what his parents did for a living, but I could tell from his tense body language in the car that it was a topic he didn't like to get into. So I didn't bring it up. Besides, what did it matter?

"The library is in there." He pointed at an open doorway behind me. I'd been expecting some stuffy, almost tacky room filled with dark leather chairs and dusty old books that were only for show. But as I walked in, I found the opposite. The room was bright and welcoming, with big, overstuffed chairs flanking a huge floor-to-ceiling window, which filled the room with warm natural light. I let my fingers trail along the bookshelves. They held everything from nonfiction to romance novels, and their spines showed signs of being read.

Evan motioned to a glass coffee table between two comfy-looking chairs. "You can put your stuff down there."

I gently dropped the backpack onto the table and sank into the nearest chair. "This room is amazing."

"I do all my homework in here."

"I'd *live* in here," I said.

"It bothers some people," he said quietly. "The money."

I met his gaze. "Well, I'm not that superficial."

He didn't say anything to that. We just stared at each other for a long moment. The butterflies in my stomach started to take flight, so I broke eye contact and pulled my backpack off the table. I unzipped it and reached inside for Flynn's notebook.

But as I went to pull it out, my portfolio came with it. I'd brought it into school to show my photography teacher the progress I'd made. It fell to the floor open, and Evan reached down to pick it up. He paused, staring at the photo on the page. One glance showed me it was the shot I'd taken of the castle at Happy Time Mini Golf. I had to explain or he'd think I was some weirdo who went back and took pictures of the place where we'd had a "moment."

"That's my portfolio," I said quickly. "It's something I work on in my spare time." I still hadn't applied for the summer course. My teacher told me my work was ready, but I couldn't pull the trigger. Maybe Toni was right. Maybe I was procrastinating because I didn't want to risk getting rejected.

"Can I look?" he asked.

I nodded, feeling self-conscious already. The only people who'd ever seen my photos were Toni and my teacher, and I think they both found them creepy.

Evan reopened the book from the beginning. The title page read:

ABANDONED RIVER'S END
Morgan Tulley

He took his time, giving each picture full consideration before slowly flipping the page. He said nothing until he was finished, and then his gray eyes found mine. Every nerve in my body was standing on edge, waiting.

"Morgan, these are amazing."

I let out an almost-too-loud breath of relief. "You think so?" Not that I would stop taking them, even if he hated them. My best friend hated them and that didn't slow me down. But for some reason, his opinion mattered to me.

"Yeah." He shook his head in amazement. "The theme kind of speaks to you, doesn't it? I mean, at first it's kind of sad. But then, and I don't know if this is what you were going for, but looking at some of these forgotten places I feel . . . hope. Like what's lost can be found again. Right?"

My ego was practically soaring. "That's exactly it."

He closed the album and handed it back to me. "Wow, these are so much better than the photos you take for the newspaper. No offense."

I laughed. "None taken. There's only so much you can do with a photo of a high school football game." I was pretty sure my cheeks were lit up like Christmas lights. I'd never felt so flattered. But then a thought occurred to me. "How did you know I take pictures for the paper?"

He shrugged. "I've seen your byline."

"You read the *River's End Weekly*?" I asked, surprised.

"No. I Googled you and it came up."

I snorted. "Stalker."

A crooked smirk played across his face. "Hey, I was just protecting myself. I was told you were dangerous, remember? You can't blame me for doing a little research after I finally found out your name at the party."

"About that . . ." I glanced down at the notebook in my lap. "Do you still have that photo of me?"

"Yeah . . . ," he said slowly. He rose and crossed to a desk in the corner. He slid open a drawer and returned a moment later with the now familiar picture in his hand, placing it writing side up on the coffee table. I opened the notebook, flipped past the messy pages, and stopped at the clean, final page. Flynn's message to me. I laid it open on the table, beside the warning.

Evan leaned forward. His breath hitched as he read the note. "This is from Flynn?" he asked.

"Yeah, but it's not the content of the note I wanted you to see. It's the handwriting."

I'd had my suspicions, but now I could verify them. I traced my finger over the capital *F* in the warning to Evan. FORGET HER. Then I compared it with the one in the notebook. *Forget me.*

They were the same.

"Flynn sent that photo to me," Evan said, confirming my thoughts out loud. "He was the one who warned me about you."

I leaned back in the chair, my mind spinning. We knew it for sure now, but it still made no sense. Flynn knew I wasn't dangerous. Why did he want Evan to stay away from me? Why did he even think we might cross paths? And why did he want me to forget him and move on?

"What's written in the rest of it?" he asked, flipping through the pages and squinting his eyes.

"Really messy notes that make no sense." I closed my eyes and let out a slow breath. "I just wish I knew what was going on."

He dropped the notebook and put his hand over mine. Our fingers interlaced. It was such a small thing, but felt so intimate. My feelings for Evan had grown from that small spark at mini golf to something bigger. Something real. But I couldn't let myself feel anything for him. Not when I still had so many questions.

"We can figure it out together," he said. But I was staring at his hand, feeling the warmth of it, the tingle it sent through my skin, wanting so much to run my thumb over his knuckles. But I didn't move.

He slid his hand back and gave me a long look. "Did you love Flynn?" he asked, and it wasn't so much hurt or jealousy in his voice as sympathy.

"No," I answered honestly. "But I might have grown to love him if . . . he'd stuck around longer." I paused, overcome with the need to share. "Can I tell you something no one knows, not even Toni?"

He met my eyes. "Of course."

I nervously licked my lips. "Right before the accident, before he got out of my car and started walking . . . he broke up with me."

Evan blew out a breath. "Well, that explains the nutty stuff in his notebook."

"How so?"

"He was clearly insane. He'd have to be crazy to dump you."

He said it with a flirty grin, and I felt like my heart was melting. I allowed my eyes to linger on the full lines of his lips. I let my mind wonder what it would feel like to have that perfect mouth on mine.

He inched forward.

My chest heaved, my breath coming faster and deeper.

"Oh! Evan, I didn't realize you had company."

Evan pulled back, his eyes widening. I sat rigidly in the chair as I turned to look at the woman in the doorway. She had that type of unmoving helmet hair you mostly see on news anchorwomen, but her smile was warm and welcoming.

"Mom, this is Morgan," Evan said.

I found my voice. "Nice to meet you, Mrs. Murphy."

She clasped her hands in front of her pale yellow pantsuit. "Likewise. Can I offer you something to drink or a snack? From the looks of it, my impolite son hasn't done so."

"Oh, sorry," Evan mumbled, as if the thought hadn't occurred to him. It hadn't occurred to me, either. We'd had . . . other things on our minds.

"Thank you," I said, "but I'm fine."

"Okay, then. I'll leave you to . . ."

"Homework," Evan finished.

"Homework," Mrs. Murphy repeated with a smile as she backed out of the room.

Evan turned to me. "Was that awkward?"

"Mildly."

He blushed a bit, then asked, "Hey, do you have any plans tonight?"

I thought about coming up with some lame line like, *Nothing I can't cancel,* so I didn't sound like a loser with no plans on a Friday night. But then I remembered the advice I'd given Reece and how well he and Toni were working out. So I went with honesty.

"No, I'm free."

He brightened. "Want to have dinner with me? Out somewhere? Like . . . not here? We can talk more about everything and try to figure out—"

"Sure," I cut in, dropping any pretense of cool.

"Great. Let's go somewhere in River's End," Evan said while I repacked my bag. "Littlefield doesn't have much."

River's End wasn't much better, but we did have Sal's. "How about pizza?" I asked.

"Perfect."

I followed Evan back down the expansive hallway, our footsteps echoing. We were almost to the door when a deep voice said, "Going out?"

Evan stopped midstride, his shoulders drooping. "Just one more introduction," he whispered to me.

"It's fine," I whispered back. I didn't mind meeting his parents. Especially since they seemed nice. This was going a lot better than it would have at my house with my parents freaking out over a dead ringer for Flynn.

We both turned around with smiles plastered on our faces, ready to do the quick meet and greet and escape to somewhere we wouldn't be interrupted.

"Dad, this is Morgan. We were just heading out for some food."

"Oh, I won't keep you, then," Mr. Murphy said brightly. His eyes took a quick scan of me, not in a creepy way, and then he gave one of those imperceptible nods to Evan that said, *Hey, she's pretty, good work.*

But I was frozen in place, like another statue for their entryway. I opened my mouth to speak, but my mind was somewhere else, and it took a moment for my lips to catch up. I finally conjured the words, "Great to meet you, Mr. Murphy."

After a quick and awkward exit, Evan opened the car door for me, then got in on the other side. He gave me a curious look. "Is something wrong?"

"No," I said quickly, though I wasn't quite sure. I needed the drive to Sal's to think. I needed to figure out if this meant anything.

Because I'd seen Evan's dad before.

CHAPTER 18
CHAPTER 18
CHAPTER 18
CHAPTER 18

CHAPTER 18

Evan held the door of Sal's open for me, and the little bell rang as the door closed again behind us. I was immediately blasted by that familiar pizza smell, and I breathed it in.

"So this is the famous Sal's, huh?" he asked.

"Yep," I said. "Fancy. Consider yourself lucky I brought you here."

"Yeah, right. I bet you take all your guys here," he joked, but I immediately felt a small pang. I *had* brought Flynn here.

At my expression, Evan quickly said, "Oh, I'm sorry. I didn't mean—"

"It's fine," I said, giving him a halfhearted smile, and the pinch in my chest disappeared.

Evan started moving toward the one open booth. My eyes made a quick sweep of the room to see if anyone I knew was there. And, lo and behold, Cooper and Diana were in the corner, holding hands over the table and making goo-goo eyes at each other.

Diana's face darkened when she saw me. I had no idea what

her problem was. She whispered something at Cooper, and he looked over his shoulder. He flashed a smile at me, but it faltered. He did a double take at my dinner companion and shot up out of his seat.

At the sight of a stranger charging toward us, Evan stepped in front of me.

"Are you . . ." Cooper's voice trailed off as he inspected him.

"No," I said, sidestepping Evan. "He just looks like him."

Cooper motioned to me with his head. "Can I talk to you for a minute?" The unspoken last word was *privately*.

Evan thankfully wasn't a jerk about it. "I'll grab the booth for us and put in an order," he said.

I told Evan what I wanted and followed Cooper back toward the doorway. He rested his elbow on the top of a gum-ball machine and looked at me expectantly.

I spread my hands. "I know this seems weird."

"I thought you'd found Flynn. I thought he was alive."

"He's not. It's not him."

"But this is why you suddenly wanted to do all that research about him."

I nodded.

He narrowed his eyes at Evan in the distance. "And you're sure he's not . . ."

"I'm sure. Flynn's dead."

Cooper shook his head and let out a low whistle. "Wow. It's uncanny."

"I know. I'm just getting used to it myself."

"Are you two . . ."

"No," I answered quickly. "He's just helping me." I glanced over my shoulder. "And you should probably head back to Diana before her head explodes." She was sitting rigidly in the booth, arms crossed, making pouty faces because Cooper's attention had gone elsewhere for one freaking minute.

"Yeah, okay. Good seeing you."

He hurried back to his corner booth, and I returned to Evan. "Sorry about that," I said, sliding into the seat, my jeans catching on the cracked vinyl. Our sodas had arrived, or rather Sal had brought over two cans from the cooler. Sal didn't have glasses. You drank from a can or you went thirsty.

I cracked mine open and took a sip, closing my eyes as the cold slipped down my throat.

"Is everything okay with that guy?" Evan asked. "Is he a jealous ex-boyfriend or something?"

I nearly spit the soda out. "Um, no. He's Toni's older brother. He thought you were Flynn, so he had a minor freakout."

"Ahh," he said, understanding. "To be expected, I guess."

"Yeah, just wait till you meet my parents." The words came out before I could stop them, and now they hung in the air like the world's most awkward and ill-placed tapestry. "Not that you'll definitely meet them. Or that there's any reason to meet them." *Shut up, Morgan.*

Evan's mouth twitched. I was glad he was fighting that laugh instead of letting it out and making me feel even more embarrassed. Good effort.

"So . . . I have something to tell you," I said, changing the subject. "I've seen your dad before."

"Oh yeah? Where?"

"Yesterday. At the falls. I was there on assignment. Someone jumped. And your dad was there, wearing a suit and looking . . . pensive."

The lighthearted expression fell from Evan's face. "It couldn't have been him."

"Why?"

"My dad doesn't go to the falls. Ever."

I pursed my lips. "If it's a fear of heights, he wasn't at the top. He was at the bottom—"

"No," Evan interrupted, "it's not that."

I smirked. "Does he have something against beautiful views?"

"That's where his brother died," he blurted.

"He . . . jumped?" Evan's uncle had committed suicide?

Evan took a long drag from his soda and nodded wordlessly.

I sank deeper into the booth. "I'm sorry."

"It's okay." He gave a small shrug.

"Maybe that's why your dad was there. Maybe he hadn't visited since . . . your uncle . . . but felt the need to after hearing the news today . . ." I let the words trail off and Evan considered them.

"Yeah, maybe. I know he hasn't dealt with Uncle Doyle's death very well. He never wants to talk about him."

"When did it happen?"

"Five years ago."

Something pinged in the back of my brain. I wanted to know more. "Did your uncle have a family?"

"No." Evan pulled a napkin from the dispenser on the table and started ripping tiny pieces from it.

"Do you know why he did it?"

He ripped one more corner off, then raised his eyes to mine. "Do you remember Stell Pharmaceuticals?"

Of course. Five years ago was when everything exploded with Stell, the plant was shut down, and everyone lost their jobs. Evan's uncle must have been another piece of Stell collateral damage. I rolled my eyes. "Say no more."

Evan returned to the napkin, his fingers slowly rolling a ripped piece back and forth along the table. "Was your family affected?"

"Yeah," I said. "My parents both worked there. And Toni's dad. They, obviously, all lost their jobs. And my friend Jennifer's parents owned the deli across the street from headquarters that went out of business soon after. I could go on and on. It seems like everyone in town was connected in some way."

I heard him swallow.

"Did your uncle work there, too?" I asked, and that part of

my brain started tingling again. I was only eleven when Stell went down and my memories were fuzzy, but this felt familiar.

Evan chewed on his lower lip and nodded.

"Did he lose everything?" I didn't know why I was pushing him. He was obviously uncomfortable. But there was something there, right under the surface, and I knew if I only scratched a little bit, it would be revealed.

"Morgan, I have to tell you something."

The bell above the door rang as Diana opened it, walking out hand in hand with Cooper, who cast one last curious glance at us before the door closed behind him.

"What?" I asked, my attention refocusing on Evan.

"One large cheese pie," Sal gruffly announced. He dropped the metal pizza pan and two paper plates in the center of the table and walked back to the counter.

Evan sucked in a breath, like he was relieved by the interruption. "We can talk about it after we eat."

"No," I said. "The pizza's too hot anyway." I separated the slices to help the cooling process, then motioned to Evan to keep talking.

He squirmed in his seat, making it even more obvious that he didn't want to tell me. But now I had to know. "Evan?" I prodded.

His eyes snapped up to mine, and I flinched at the fear I saw in them. What was he scared of? What was his secret?

His gaze went distant as he began to speak. "My family is

responsible for all of this unhappiness—in your family, in Toni's, in all your other friends. The small businesses that shut down. The abandoned places you visit. It's all because of us."

Panic had started to edge his voice, so I reached across the table and laid my hand over his. "Evan, slow down. What are you talking about?"

A sort of depressed resignation settled into his normally bright eyes. "My family owned Stell."

I pulled my hands back. "What?"

"My father was the CFO, the chief financial officer. My uncle was the CEO, the head of the company."

I remembered now. The CEO had committed suicide. My parents didn't let me watch morbid stuff like that on the news at that age, but kids talk on the playground. He was one of the falls' many jumpers.

And Evan was his family.

Evan continued, "My dad just handled the money, but my uncle ran the business. He knew about the deaths tied to the migraine pill. He covered it up, kept producing the drug. Then when the whistleblower blew the lid off the whole thing and Stell was put out of business . . . Doyle's life was pretty much over. My dad lost his job, too, even though he did nothing wrong. He'll probably never be a CFO again, but he does independent consulting now, here and there, traveling to other firms and helping them buy out other companies or whatever.

But Uncle Doyle was done. He was going to face charges. So he . . . did what he did . . . at the falls."

That now-familiar anger I'd felt over and over again throughout the years surfaced, reddening my cheeks. The leaders of Stell had always been these nameless mythical villains in my head. People I could blame without having to see or talk to them. But now, here was Evan. His last name, Murphy, was so commonplace here in Irish Massachusetts, I never would have connected him to some CEO who died when I was in elementary school. I hadn't even remembered the guy's name. But Evan should have told me.

"Why didn't you mention this before?" I asked.

His voice was tight. "Because I didn't want you to look at me the way you're looking at me right now. The way my classmates look at me. At all of us. That's why my sister goes to boarding school. She couldn't handle it."

That's why he was wary of bringing me home. Why he drove a cheap, unassuming car.

"So why are you telling me now?" I asked.

"Because I don't want to keep any secrets from you." His eyes implored mine to believe him.

My insides twisted as I absorbed the information. It was unfair of me to lay anything on Evan. He was only a kid when everything happened, just like me. It wasn't his fault. And he'd clearly suffered for Stell's wrongdoings as well.

He leaned forward. "What are you thinking? Please, just tell me."

I opened my backpack and slid Flynn's notebook out. "Now that I know this, I should share something else with you."

Evan looked confused. "You already showed me Flynn's note."

True. But now, I realized, the rest of it was relevant, too. "The messy notes he wrote in the rest of the book," I began. "They were about your family's company. He seemed to be . . . researching it."

Evan blinked rapidly in surprise. "Why?"

"That's what I plan to find out." I hesitated. "And I guess I need to know if you're still with me."

Evan took the notebook from my hands and wordlessly flipped through it, stopping to squint and run his fingers over certain words and names. After what seemed like forever, he handed it back to me, his jaw set rigidly, his eyes burning with determination.

Through clenched teeth, he answered, "Definitely."

CHAPTER 19

As far as I knew, Toni had never been interested in attending a high school baseball game in her natural-born life. But now that she was dating the first baseman, she'd suddenly been infected with a giant case of school spirit, and here we were.

On my way out to the field, I had swung by the library and photocopied the notes from Flynn's journal. Evan wanted to inspect the notebook more, but I wasn't about to part with it. So I filled my pocket with dimes and let the copy machine do its work. Then I headed to the game.

Toni was already sitting on the bleachers when I got there, cheering like one of those crazy parents who took things too seriously.

"You call that a strike?" she yelled.

I slid in next to her and gave her the side-eye.

"What?" she asked.

"Nothing." I returned my eyes to the field and clapped when our player got a single. But I could feel Toni's stare on the side of my head.

"You think it's happening again," she said.

"I think what's happening again?"

"The crazy."

"Oh. *That.*"

She crossed her arms and made a huffing sound. "Morgan. I know it's fast. But I like him."

"I'm not saying anything, Toni. You're arguing with no one here."

"But I know you're thinking it. You're judging me with your thoughts."

"Then why don't your thoughts fight my thoughts and we can just do this all telepathically?"

She pushed closer to me on the bleacher. "Why don't you want to talk about it?"

"Because you already have your mind made up, and I don't want to fight. I want to watch the game. It's thrilling. Isn't this thrilling?" I pointed to the field, where absolutely nothing was happening. We had a guy on first base, but the pitcher was taking about ninety seconds between each throw. He must've been some kind of obsessive compulsive, because he did this hat-adjust-spit-kick-at-the-mound combination over and over again until he felt comfortable enough to toss the next pitch.

"Watching a goat eat grass would be more exciting," Toni said.

I gave her a look that said *duh.* "Then why are we here?"

"Because I want to cheer him on. It makes him feel good to

know I'm here. And it makes me feel good that he's glad I'm here. And it's this big feel-good circle and what's wrong with feeling good?"

I thought about Evan and how I felt when I was close to him. My heart raced, my throat dried up, my skin felt electric. And I was pushing the possibility of him—of us—away. Maybe I just wasn't ready. I didn't know. All I knew was that I wished I could be carefree like Toni and just throw my heart into it. Let myself feel what I desperately wanted to. Stop holding back.

"Nothing's wrong with feeling good," I admitted. I smiled and bumped her shoulder with mine. "Go for it. Do your boy-crazy thing."

Her eyes were glassy. She looked both fearful and deliriously happy at the same time—if that was possible. "And if it crashes and burns?" she asked.

I let out a little sigh. "Then I'll be here to pick up the pieces. With a giant bag of Sour Patch Kids to dull the pain."

"I love you, Morgan."

"I am the bestest best friend in all of best friend land."

"Yes, you are."

The bleachers erupted into cheers as one of our players hit a home run. I mock bowed as if they were cheering for me, and Toni nearly fell over laughing.

When the game quickly returned to boring, Toni kicked the backpack at my feet. "Why do you have that with you?"

"I had to stop at the library and copy Flynn's notebook for Evan."

She wagged her eyebrows. "Oh, *really*. Apparently you've been holding out on me. Deets. Now."

I filled her in on the events of last night. Sharing the journal with Evan, dinner at Sal's, and learning that Evan's family had owned Stell.

Toni took in a sharp breath. "Wow. So . . . his family ruined our lives."

"It's not that simple. And it's not *his* fault."

"Still. It's very *Romeo and Juliet*. You're dating the enemy."

I groaned. "One: we're not dating. Two: he's not the enemy. He was just a kid like us when Stell went down."

"Why do you always have to undramatize everything?" she teased.

"Why do you always have to *over*dramatize everything?" I shot back.

She snorted. "So what's your next step? Now that you and Romeo are working together."

I took a deep breath. "I don't know. I pored over the journal myself and I can't figure out anything. It just seems like a bunch of unconnected names and dates to me. I'm hoping Evan might see something I don't."

Toni tapped her chin for a moment. "You know who knows the most about the Stell thing?"

I shrugged. "Who?"

"Cooper."

"How would he know?"

"He based all his college application essays on it. The company going down, the town quickly following. You know, for these essays you have to use whatever hits you've taken. Our family took one from Stell. So he figured why not turn around and use that sob story to his advantage? He did a ton of research so he'd have all the facts right before he wrote his essay."

"Maybe I'll talk to him." I logged that into my mental to-do list.

"Wait until Monday. Diana's home for the weekend. No one can pry him away from her." Toni rolled her eyes as she said it.

"I know. He talked to me for thirty seconds at Sal's and I thought she was going to spontaneously combust."

We watched the rest of the game, cheering when appropriate and gabbing the remainder of the time. I still didn't find baseball any more exciting by the end, but it was nice to just sit and chat with Toni. I missed her when we went a few days without quality time, and we'd both had so much going on lately.

River's End edged out the other team by two runs, and Toni ran into Reece's arms like he'd won the World Series.

"The team is heading to Sal's for some celebratory eats," Reece said. "You two in?"

Toni oozed enthusiasm. "I'm in!"

I appreciated the fact that Reece had included me, even

though there was clearly only one person who mattered. "I'm out, guys. I have to drop those papers off to Evan before *his* baseball game starts."

Reece brightened. "Hey, you should go watch his game!"

"Not today." At Toni's disappointed look, I smirked and added, "But maybe someday."

Twenty minutes later, I was pulling into the front gates of the palace, or rather, Evan's house. I sent him a text, and he came running down the driveway in full gear—Littlefield uniform, hat, and cleats. Either I hadn't stopped to appreciate the snug fit of the sport's uniforms at the game earlier today or Evan just filled his out better. My eyes traveled down from his upper arms to his muscular thighs, all stretching the seams of the tight material. *Damn.*

He came up to the driver's-side window. "Yeah, I know. I look dorky," he said, catching my stare.

"No, um, not at all. You look . . . fine. Um, I mean, okay," I bumbled. I opened my book bag and nearly shoved my head inside of it to cover up the blush creeping across my cheeks. I pulled out the photocopied pages and handed them out the car window. "Here it is."

"Thanks." He rolled the pages up and shoved them into his back pocket. "I'm sorry I can't look at it today. It's just that I missed one practice this week already, and—"

"No worries," I cut in, wondering if that practice he'd missed was because he'd been with me. "I have a lot of homework to catch up on anyway. Just call me when you get a chance to read through it."

"I will." He smiled.

"And good luck at your game."

"Thanks." He made no motion to walk away. As if he were waiting for me to give him a reason to stay.

I glanced at the clock on my dashboard. "You're going to be late."

That snapped him out of it. "Yeah, you're right. I'll call you!" He waved and ran up the driveway. And I totally didn't take my time leaving so I could watch him. Nope, not at all.

When I finally pulled away, my mind was dizzy with endorphins or whatever chemical makes your brain go loopy at the thought of a particular guy. I always tiptoed through life so carefully. Maybe I should just be reckless like Toni. Throw caution to the wind. What's the worst that could happen? Yeah, I could get hurt. But I'd been hurt before, and I lived through it.

I didn't notice the SUV behind me until I stopped at a light. It was so close, its front grille could have been in my trunk.

What the hell? I thought. How about giving me some breathing room?

The light turned green. I accelerated a little faster than I normally would, but the SUV kept right on top of me, only inches from my bumper. Close enough to hit me if I had to

slam on the brakes. Aggravated, I pushed the pedal down far-
ther, definitely speeding now, but at least it put a little distance
between us.

I glanced in the side mirror and realized . . . it was a *black*
SUV. The boxy kind—a very familiar shape.

My skin prickled, the hairs on my arms standing stiff as
needles.

Just a coincidence, I told myself. A lot of people drive black
SUVs. Just because I was noticing them now didn't mean they
were all the same car. Plus, in movies when people are being
followed, the car is always careful about it, staying a good distance behind. If this person was following me, they weren't
even bothering to hide it. It was more like they *wanted* me to
know. Like they wanted to scare me.

I let up on the gas and slowed back down to the speed limit.
Paranoia wasn't worth a hundred-dollar speeding ticket. The
SUV caught up. I squinted in my rearview mirror, hoping to
catch a glimpse of a face. But the windows were tinted.

I went straight through the stop sign on North Street and
took a left onto Blueberry Road. The SUV followed. Blueberry
was a residential road that made a giant letter "C" leading right
back to North Street a half mile down. I reached the end and
made a right onto North. I'd made a useless circle, but the SUV
still stayed close behind.

I approached the next intersection as the light turned red.
It had two lanes. I took the right one. I glanced in the rearview

again and the SUV was gone. But before I could let out a breath of relief, it pulled up slowly into the left lane beside me, stopping parallel to my car.

I hit the automatic door-lock button with my elbow. But no one got out. The window didn't roll down. There was no clear threat.

I stared through my driver's-side window and saw nothing. The SUV's darkened glass was impenetrable, but I knew— *knew*—the person inside was staring back at me. I felt it in every cell of my body. Fear's icy fingers tiptoed down my spine, and some basic instinct in my DNA made my breaths come faster, my heart pump wilder.

The light turned green. I paused. The SUV didn't make a move, as if waiting for me. Home was straight, but there was no way I was leading this psychopath right to my front door. I jerked the wheel to the right and floored it, my tires screeching.

I made the turn, my back wheels fishtailing a bit, and saw the SUV following. It had taken a right turn from the left lane. There was no chance this person was lost. This was not my overactive imagination.

On Main Street now, I had to be careful. I couldn't go too fast or spend too much time with my eyes on the mirror. This was the busy center of town. Cars pulled out of street spots quickly, and people jaywalked.

My mind raced, wondering what to do. I couldn't go home, but I didn't want to lead this person to Toni's, either. If I kept driving, we'd eventually end up somewhere deserted, and who knew what would happen. I gripped the wheel so tightly, my knuckles started to ache.

Then, suddenly, the answer appeared, like a beacon in front of me. I slammed on the brakes and took a right into the small parking lot of the River's End Police Department. There were no spots left except the handicapped one in front, but I took that. Let someone come out and ticket me. *Please.*

I turned and looked out my back window. The SUV had come to a complete stop in the road.

"Checkmate, jackass," I said out loud.

The front door of the police station opened and a uniformed officer walked out. "Miss? You can't park there."

I rolled the window down. "Sorry, Officer. I wasn't planning to stay. It's just that someone was following me."

The cop's face hardened. "In a vehicle?"

"Yes, that black SUV." I pointed toward the road, but of course by now the car was gone. "It went past," I said, shaking my head.

"Because you were smart enough to pull in here," the officer complimented me. "Was this a road-rage incident?"

"No, the car was just . . . following me."

At that point, his expression changed. I knew he was wondering if I was just some paranoid girl.

"Did you get the plate?" he asked.

"There wasn't one on the front and he was behind me. I couldn't see the back."

The officer exhaled loudly through his nose. "Well, you can stay here awhile until you feel safe enough to head on home. If you run into trouble again, come back."

I wanted to ask the officer to stay with me, to stand sentinel beside my car. But he trudged back into the station. I knew he thought I was crazy. But I was sure something else was going on. I only wished I'd been paying attention from the start. Where had the SUV picked up my tail? From Evan's house? And more important, why?

After ten minutes, I felt it was safe to pull out. I didn't go straight to my house. I made crazy turns and circles to make sure the SUV hadn't been waiting for me somewhere. When I was sure I was no longer being followed, I headed home and pulled into the driveway behind my parents' cars.

My nerves were starting to return to normal, but I still clutched my stomach as I walked up the front path. In a snap decision, I knew I wouldn't tell my parents about the SUV. They would probably freak out and make me stay home all the time. It would cause more trouble than it was worth. By nature, I liked to avoid any conversation that might lead to an argument. Life was easier that way.

I paused before opening the front door. I'd always thought my parents and I were close because we didn't fight. But I was starting to see that just because we pretended everything was all right, that didn't mean we were staying close. Maybe we were actually pushing each other away. Widening the chasm between us.

Maybe it was time for that to change.

I took a deep breath and threw open the door. Just in time to hear my mother scream.

CHAPTER 20

"**M**organ!" Mom yelled. One hand was against her cheek and the other clutched a piece of paper to her chest. "You scared me."

"Sorry," I said, closing the door quietly behind me.

"Why can't you open the door like a normal person?" Mom complained. "You basically tried to blow it off its hinges."

She stood in the living room, her back to the darkened television, facing Dad. What had they been doing? Not watching TV. And, strangely, Dad's face was pale and withdrawn.

Although sudden noises always startled Mom, they never affected Dad. My whole life, any time I dropped something or inadvertently came around a corner too quickly, Mom would scream and jump as if she'd been given an electrical shock, but Dad never reacted. Except to laugh at Mom's antics.

Right now, though, he looked frightened.

"Did I scare you, too?" I asked.

"Not at all." He shrugged. But his eyes darted to Mom. To the paper she held against her chest.

"What's that?"

Mom looked down, only now realizing that I could see whatever it was she had grasped in her hand. She slowly folded the paper in half. "Just a bill that we're going to protest. The cable company made a mistake again."

An unspoken look passed between them.

I held out my hand. "Can I see it?"

Dad turned toward me, surprised that I'd made a move.

Mom said sweetly, "Don't waste your time, honey. We've got it."

I matched her sugarcoated tone. "But I might be able to help you figure out the problem."

Mom gave me a tight smile. "We know what the problem is. We just have to make a phone call during office hours." She waited for me to let it go and wander off, but I stood my ground, silently letting her know I wouldn't be brushed off.

"There's Chinese takeout in the kitchen," she said with finality.

Something was going on. This was more than a little argument and frantic whispering in the night. They were keeping something big from me.

In the past, I would've walked away as told. Comfortable in the knowledge that my parents would handle whatever it was and I didn't have to worry about it. I wasn't a meddler and respected people's privacy. Maybe that's why Flynn's mysterious nature never bothered me. But now . . . that didn't seem good enough anymore. I didn't want to be left in the dark—by a boyfriend or my parents.

I straightened my shoulders. "I want to know what's going on."

Mom rolled her eyes in faux annoyance. "Oh, Morgan. Everything that happens in the world doesn't have to do with you."

I simmered with frustration, but kept my voice level. "I'm not saying it does. I just think, if something's going on with my *family*, it should involve me. Am I right?"

I looked at Dad. He averted his eyes, like if he didn't look at me, he wouldn't have to answer my questions.

"Looking away doesn't wrap you in an invisibility cloak, Dad." The bitterness in my voice shocked even me. Dad bristled. If he had been a porcupine, I would've been stabbed by a hundred needles.

"Morgan," Mom said sharply. "Tantrums didn't work on us when you were two and they won't work now. Go to the kitchen and eat something for dinner or go to your room. Enough of this. I don't know what's gotten into you."

I could have pounded my feet against the hardwood floor and started screaming—a real tantrum—but it wasn't worth expending the energy. I knew when I'd hit the Brick Wall of Mom.

"Fine," I muttered. Then I turned the corner into the kitchen and grabbed the cardboard container of vegetable lo mein, a fork, and a can of soda. I made sure to let them see me, arms awkwardly full, before I started up the staircase. When I reached the second floor, I placed the dinner on my desk, then backed out of my room and slammed the door. They'd think I was in there, shoving noodles into my pouty face.

Instead, I crept back to the stairwell, knelt down on the floor behind the wall, and peeked my head around. This was usually a good spot to listen from because they wouldn't see me unless they came to the bottom of the steps. It was something I hadn't done since I was a little girl.

Mom and Dad were still in the living room, speaking in hushed whispers, their voices rising only now and then.

"I don't know what to do, either!" Mom hissed. "But we can't just . . ."

Though I strained to hear, the rest was unintelligible.

Dad, sounding completely hopeless, said, "We'll talk about this later."

Later meaning after I was asleep. After there was no chance I would overhear them.

Not tonight, folks, I thought. *I can stay up as late as I need to.*

"What should we do with—" Mom started.

"Burn it," Dad hissed. I heard him stalk off. I pulled my head back until he passed, then listened again.

But Mom didn't follow. I took a risk and inched my butt down two steps. I peeked my head through the balusters.

Mom stood alone, her shoulders drooping, as she stared at the floor, that mysterious paper still clutched in her hand. My heart cinched. I wanted to say, *Whatever it is, we'll get through it. As a family. Just let me in.*

I watched as she selected a hardcover from the bookcase, slipped the paper inside, and replaced the book. I memorized its position—middle row, third book. Then I snuck back to my room.

Though I was barely hungry, I forced myself to eat some of the noodles, then plopped back on my bed. I just had to wait my parents out and then I'd see what the big secret was. But what to do in the meantime? Toni was probably busy with Reece. I had no desire to start my homework. I couldn't concentrate on a novel. I turned on my TV. After a while my phone started chirping from my bag.

I pulled it out. A text from Evan. My heart did a little flip.

want to talk?

I typed back: sure. call me.

Almost immediately my phone lit up with his reply.

im outside your house.

I thought about inviting him in. It wasn't too late. But the rational part of me immediately vetoed the idea. I could already picture the drama in my head. My father's confused face. My mother's high-pitched inquisition. *Why does he look exactly like Flynn? Are they related? Where did you meet? What's going on?*

No, thanks. My drama cup already runneth over.

I wrote back: park at the end of the road. i'll be there in 5.

I shook my hair out, pulled on a hoodie, and headed downstairs. Mom was in the living room, paging through a magazine on the couch. I'd been hoping to take a quick peek at the mystery paper she'd hidden in the bookcase, but that would obviously have to wait.

"Where are you going?" she asked, noticing me creep toward the front door.

"Walking to Toni's." Before she could start in on how she didn't want me around Toni's parents, I added, "Her parents aren't home. We're just going to hang out with Cooper for a little bit."

I'd never blatantly lied to my parents before. By omission, of course: that was my family's modus operandi. But I figured they were lying to me, so why not start?

"Have fun." Mom returned her attention to the magazine, and I walked out the door. She was probably happy to have me and my questions gone for the night.

A quick shower had passed through, and the pavement was damp. My sneakers slapped against the sidewalk as I strode by my neighbors' darkened houses. I glanced at their pulled shades and wondered what secrets they hid behind them. It was becoming apparent to me that every family had their own.

Evan's car was parked at the end of the street. The lights were off, and I could barely make out his shadow in the driver's seat. I opened the passenger-side door and slid in. The interior light came on, casting an orange glow over his features. He hadn't even taken his uniform off yet, just turned the hat backward. His right leg was stained with dirt from a slide or a stolen base.

He squinted, but reached up to click the button and keep the light on. "How's it going?" he asked, not looking at me.

Weird. The car was parked. He didn't need to have his eyes glued to the road. "It hasn't been the greatest day in the world," I answered.

He unrolled the photocopied pages and spread them open on his lap. "After my game, I spent a lot of time poring over Flynn's journal."

"And?" I prodded.

He flipped through the pages. "I recognize some of the names. And I cross-referenced the dates. They seem to be important."

"Like what?" I asked.

"The date the story broke about Stell. The date the company went down. The date my uncle died." He ran a hand across his forehead. "I just don't understand the point of the notes."

It seemed obvious to me. "Clearly, Flynn thought something was rotten in the land of Stell."

"And he was right. But that's what I'm trying to say. What was his goal here? To bring down Stell? To ruin my family's name? All that happened already, years ago."

My nerves prickled. Why did Evan jump to the conclusion that Flynn was out to destroy something? "Just because he was researching Stell, that doesn't mean he had bad intentions. What about the fact that he looked just like you? That can't be a coincidence."

He ran his finger up and down the edge of the pages. "Yeah, I've thought a lot about that, too. Maybe he was a distant cousin I didn't know about. Maybe he thought he could come here and try to, I don't know, squeeze some money from us or something?"

"Or maybe he just wanted to understand what happened," I chimed in.

He looked up at me, surprised. "People don't go through this amount of effort out of curiosity. He wanted something. I just don't know why he was digging through the past." He paused. "Maybe he was working on a book, a tell-all?"

"He was a teenager, Evan." The words came out snappier than I'd intended.

"I don't know. I'm just throwing ideas out there," he said, his voice tight as a fist. "Do you have any better ones?"

That your parents are hiding something, I thought. *Just like mine.* But I pressed my lips together before the words could escape. Evan wasn't himself. He seemed frustrated. Tension had settled into his neck and shoulders, and a worry line formed between his brows.

"Are you okay?" I asked.

His eyes found mine, and he let out a long breath. "I'm sorry," he said. "I didn't mean to snap at you."

"What is it?"

He heaved a sigh. "It took a long time for me to put this Stell stuff behind me. You know how many kids at school blamed me for their problems? Because their parents lost their jobs and stuff. It's only now, five years later, that people seem to be starting to forget about it. And here I am reading all this. It just brings back memories."

He gave me a weary smile, but it felt like a punch to the stomach. I'd been so selfish. I was only thinking about me. My driving need to figure out the mystery that was Flynn. I had never stopped for a moment to think about how hard this might be for Evan.

"You don't have to be involved in this—" I started.

"Yes, I do," he said. "I'm in this, whether I like it or not. Your boyfriend looked just like me. He sent me a picture of you. He kept a notebook about my family."

"About your family's *company*," I corrected.

"Same thing. We're always going to be linked."

I paused, not knowing how to word a possibly sensitive question. "Did your dad know? About the cover-up?"

"He swears he didn't, and there's no evidence that he did. He says Uncle Doyle never told him. Those studies never came across his desk. He just dealt with the finances."

I sensed a *but*... "But you don't believe him?"

"I don't know what to believe. I just . . . I know when my dad is keeping a secret, and he's been keeping a big one for a while. He gets shifty sometimes."

"How do you mean?"

"He has days, weeks even, when he's a nervous wreck. But he denies it. Then it passes and he's regular old Dad for a few months, but it always happens again."

I thought about Toni's family and how the layoff had affected them. And how even my own parents had had their shifty moments lately. "Maybe it's anxiety or depression," I said. "Losing his company, losing his brother."

"Yeah, that's what my mom thinks."

Another thought whispered from the back of my mind, latching on to the memory of Mr. Murphy at the falls, staring at the water. His brother had destroyed their company. He must've been pretty angry about that. Angry enough to kill?

Evan sighed. "I wanted this to be over, you know? For our family to move on. But it seems like it will never be over."

His tone was so bleak. I hated that I'd dragged him into this and dredged up old pain. Almost without thinking, I reached out and touched his shoulder. Not caring if I was sending him the wrong message.

His eyes closed, and I took the opportunity to unabashedly stare at him, the lines of his jaw, the curve of his lips. If he looked at me now, I wouldn't be able to stop myself from kissing him.

He opened his eyes, but stared straight ahead.

I grudgingly pulled my hand back to my lap.

"Sorry I'm such bad company tonight," he said softly. "I want to help you with this. We *will* get to the bottom of it. I just . . . It's a little overwhelming right now."

"Okay." I didn't want to leave the warmth of his car. I didn't want to leave *him*. But he needed me to. He needed to get home, to think, to sleep.

"I'll be in a better mood the next time. I promise." He gave me a weak smile.

"Talk to you later," I said, and slipped into the night.

I trekked back down the road. Evan didn't pull away until he saw me safely reach the walk in front of my house. I watched his taillights turn the corner and vanish.

I used my key in the front door and closed it quietly behind me. The living room was empty. My heart sped up. If my parents were asleep, now was the time. But my hope came crashing down with the clink of silverware in the kitchen.

I pulled my sneakers off and padded into the room. Dad was seated at the table, hunched over a bowl.

He looked up and tried to give me a smile. "Ice cream?"

I leaned my shoulder against the wall. "No, thanks."

This was what my dad did after arguments. He tried to smooth things over by buying me ice cream or a new book by my favorite author, or by offering me the remote and letting me pick what show we'd watch. Little things. Sweet things.

But things that ignored the problem. And I felt like, if I took his peace offering, it was a tacit acceptance that the issue was handled.

"I'm not hungry," I said, and headed into the living room.

I settled onto the couch, my legs tucked underneath me, and pretended to be absorbed in the magazine my mom had left behind. But Dad didn't seem to notice how little I truly cared about it as he stopped at the bottom of the staircase.

"Good night," he said.

"Good night," I echoed.

"Don't stay up too late."

"I won't."

I listened closely as his footfalls echoed up the staircase. The second floor creaked under his weight. The door to their bedroom clicked shut.

I quietly approached the bookcase. My fingers trailed along the spines and stopped at the book I'd seen my mother with. I eased it off the shelf and flipped through until I found the mystery paper. Still there.

I slipped it out of the book. I didn't know what I was expecting. Something bad, obviously. But ripples of anxiety shuddered through me as I wondered just how bad it would be. An overdue statement? A foreclosure warning? I closed my eyes and breathed deeply. Part of me wanted to put the paper back and pretend it didn't exist. But that was the old Morgan. No more keeping my head in the sand.

I unfolded the paper and saw that it was actually a note. Not a bill. Not a formal letter. It was handwritten, with big, menacing block letters. Like Flynn's warning to Evan. But this wasn't Flynn's handwriting. I knew that well enough now. The statement was simple and to the point.

EVERYONE WILL KNOW WHAT YOU DID.

What the hell? I hadn't been expecting anything like this. Was this for my parents?

What had they done?

CHAPTER 21

CHAPTER 21
CHAPTER 21
CHAPTER 21
CHAPTER 21

Sunday morning, I woke to the warmth of the sun on my face. I'd forgotten to pull the curtains before I'd collapsed into bed. I lay there for a while, listening to the birds outside, and thinking about the time, a few years ago, when we had a leaky pipe in the kitchen.

My dad had been on his hands and knees on the floor, head under the sink. I sat beside him, passing a tool now and then and feeling impatient because we were supposed to go out. I was amazed by how much effort he was putting in—using a wrench, pliers, tape, sealant. "That's good enough," I said. "Can't we just go?"

And Dad replied, "Not yet. If there's one loose seal, even the tiniest crack, the water will find it. Water always finds a way out."

Watching the patterns of light dance on my bedroom wall now, I realized that secrets were like water. They slipped around, hidden, searching for that one small crack.

And they always found a way out.

Flynn took his lies to the grave, but left behind his journal.

My parents refused to admit there was a problem, but the note I found proved it. And Evan's family?

Sometimes secrets revealed themselves, but other times you had to give them a little push.

I slid out of bed, showered, and got ready. My parents were out. I hated this rift forming between us. Whatever they were hiding, I was sure they thought they were protecting me. But I didn't want to be protected. I wanted the truth. However bitter it would taste going down, it had to be better than these lies I'd been spoon-fed.

I grabbed my car keys and went outside. It was the first warm day of spring. Mom's tulips had started to open. I kept the car window down as I drove past neighbors working outside, mowing lawns, washing cars. I parked in Toni's driveway.

Toni had two laughs. Her real laugh, the one I heard most often. And her boyfriend laugh, the one she reserved for guys who told her a joke and she wanted to make them feel good. That laugh was so loud, you didn't so much hear it as feel assaulted by it. And that's how I knew that she was out on the back deck and she wasn't alone.

I strode around the side of the house. Toni and Reece were lounging in chairs on the sun-bleached deck, sipping lemonade.

She brightened when she saw me. "Morgan! Come pull up a chair. It's beautiful out."

"There's nice scenery all right," Reece said, ogling Toni in her tank top.

Toni gave him a playful smack on the arm. "Go in and get her a glass of lemonade."

Reece jumped up and opened the sliding glass door. I waited for him to close it before I turned to Toni. "I came to ask you to do something with me."

"Sure!" she said, enthusiasm shooting out of her pores. "What do you want to do?"

I smiled slowly. "Break into Evan's house."

She paused, the glass halfway to her mouth. "Did your brain dribble out of your ears overnight?"

"His parents are hiding something. I know it. And I don't know if Evan's willing to do what it takes to find the truth. So I need to find it myself."

Toni put the glass down on a side table. "Humoring you for a moment. How would we even do this?"

"Evan has another game today, at noon. We stake out his house and see if his parents go to watch him play. His little sister's away at boarding school. The house would be empty."

Toni shook her head. "With a house like that, they definitely have an alarm system."

I grinned. "I know a way in."

She rubbed her chin. "Okay, I'm intrigued," she admitted.

"Will you do it?" I eyeballed Reece through the window. He was getting ice from the freezer. I had to get Toni to agree before he came out and acted like the voice of reason.

Toni let out an unsure sigh. "I don't know."

"Just so you know, I'm doing it with or without you. And I was kind of hoping you would come since we haven't spent much time together lately."

Toni winced. That one got her. She knew she'd been blowing me off for Reece, and I was betting that she felt guilty about it. It was a low blow, but desperate times, desperate measures.

She sat up in her chair. "I have conditions. One: we don't involve Reece. I don't want to get him in trouble."

"Adorable."

"Two," she continued. "If we don't physically see everyone leaving the premises, we abort the mission, and you never bring this up again."

I chewed on my lip. "All or nothing, huh?"

She crossed her arms forcefully. "Yep."

"Deal." I could always go back by myself some other time.

The sliding glass door opened, and Reece came out with my lemonade. The ice cubes clinked against the glass as I took a long, satisfying sip.

With one last glance at me, Toni said to Reece, "We're going to head out around eleven thirty for some girl time." She hesitated a beat. "Shopping."

"I feel guilty." Toni slumped down in the driver's seat. We were parked on the street outside Evan's house. We'd taken Cooper's car because Evan wouldn't recognize it.

"For lying to Reece about where we were going?" I asked.

"Yeah. Couples shouldn't lie to each other." She bulged her eyes out at me with a silent but not subtle message.

"Evan and I are not a couple. And I'm not lying to him."

"Just breaking into his house," she mumbled.

"You shouldn't feel guilty," I said, turning the subject back around. "You're protecting Reece. It's cute."

She gave me a skeptical look.

"Who knows, maybe you'll learn some tips that will help him conquer that King Mother house he wants to throw a party in."

She stiffened. "Here comes a car."

I followed her gaze up the long driveway. Only one car was making its way down. Damn, I thought. I needed them all to go to the game. But then it got to the bottom of the drive and I realized it wasn't Evan's car. It was a sleek black sedan. And as it turned onto the road, I counted three heads: two in the front, Evan's in the back. They'd all left together.

I grinned. "Time to go."

We easily slipped through the iron bars of the gate surrounding the property, making me think it was more ornamental than protective. I hiked up the hill, Toni two steps behind me. The Murphys owned so much property, there wasn't a neighbor who could see us, but we jogged just in case.

Toni groaned. "I feel like I'm in a James Bond movie. I shouldn't feel like that, Morgan. I should be drinking lemonade on my deck."

"Zip it."

"It's not too late to turn into a sane person."

I glanced over my shoulder. She gave me a withering look, and I realized she was scared. But she'd cover it up with one-liners and keep going if I wanted her to.

"Why don't you go back to the car?" I suggested. "Be the lookout."

Instead of grabbing the chance, Toni actually looked of-fended. "You're trying to get rid of me," she accused. "You think I'm going to mess this up!"

"No, I don't. I was just thinking—"

"You're not getting rid of me, Morgan. I'm great at this stuff. I'm a ninja." She pushed past me in a huff.

"How are we going to get in?" Toni asked once we reached the back of the house.

"Evan mentioned that the den window isn't wired to the alarm system right now. They had to replace it. So I just have to find the den."

Toni pointed at one window whose frame was a brighter white than the others, like it was more freshly painted. "How about that one?"

I stepped into the landscaping and squeezed between two bushes. The window definitely looked new. I cupped my hands to peer through the glass. The room inside had a bookcase and a desk—looked like the den.

"This must be it," I said.

I'd been hoping the windows would be open, it being the first warm day and all. But they weren't. I made a deal with myself. If the den window was locked, I'd leave it at that. Walk away. But if I could open it, well, then that was an invitation from fate. It wasn't breaking and entering if I didn't have to break anything to get in . . . right?

I pushed up against the sill. The window groaned . . . and opened.

I looked back at Toni.

"Last chance," she said. "Are you sure you want to do this?"

I'd been repeating the words *it's not too late to back out* to myself for the last hour, like a mantra. They made me feel better. What I was doing was clearly crazy, but if I could still back out, there was no reason to be scared.

We were here now, though. The Murphys were gone. The window was open. There was no backing out. Not anymore. I put a finger to my lips so Toni would stop trying to talk me out of it. Panic desperately wanted to settle into my bones, but I pushed past it. I had to get answers.

The screen slid up easily. I motioned to Toni.

"Me?" she said, aghast. "Why do I have to go first?"

"Because I'm tall enough to climb in myself without a boost. You're not."

"Stupid DNA," she growled.

I locked my fingers together to form a step and Toni put one foot onto it, then pulled herself up to the ledge and through the window. Her face popped back up a moment later and I breathed a sigh of relief. With a little maneuvering, I grabbed the ledge, got some traction with my feet on the siding, and pulled myself up and in, careful not to make too much noise when I dropped to the floor.

I stood up and let my eyes adjust. Toni was already wandering around the unfamiliar room. It was very masculine, with leather furniture and a large mahogany desk. It wasn't just a den. It was Mr. Murphy's office.

Toni pointed at the huge, imposing chair behind the desk. "I want to sit in that, facing the other way, then spin around slowly and say something evil. Like in the movies."

"Maybe next time," I said. "You take the left drawers, I'll take the right."

She snorted. "You're no fun."

The first drawer slid open easily. I flipped through the stack of papers. They seemed like regular business documents, some invoices, bills, stuff like that. The bottom drawer had file folders that were all labeled with company names. Nothing that looked personal. Evan said his dad did consulting now. That's all this was.

"Anything?" I asked Toni.

"Nothing secret-y, no. Let's go."

"Not yet," I said.

Toni groaned. "What are you expecting to find? A hidden birth certificate? A secret diary?"

Secrets have a way of revealing themselves. "I don't know. Just look."

I went over to a tall bookcase against the wall. One shelf held framed photos. Evan and his sister. The whole family. One of just Evan and his mom. One of his father and uncle— identical aside from Evan's uncle's beard. I picked up a small frame and froze.

"Toni," I whispered.

She hurried to my side. "What is it?"

With a trembling hand, I gave her the frame. "Look. There's Evan, about age one or two. And his mom is pregnant."

Toni sighed and put the photo back in its place. "Settle down, conspira-zilla. Didn't you say he has a younger sister? That's her baking in there."

"Oh, yeah." I felt stupid for not realizing it immediately. What was wrong with me?

I caught Toni staring. "What?"

She chewed on her lip. "If I say something, will you promise not to take it the wrong way?"

"No."

Toni rolled her eyes. "Fine, I'll say it anyway. I think you want there to be something here. Some big conspiracy waiting to be unearthed."

I crossed my arms. "And why's that, Dr. Toni?"

"Because maybe then Flynn's death wouldn't seem so senseless."

I inhaled sharply and turned around. I felt sucker punched.

Toni put a gentle hand on my arm. "I'm sorry. I shouldn't have said—"

"No, you're right." I turned to face her. "I should just admit it. I don't want his death to have been random. Me picking him up, us fighting, him walking down the road, the car coming. I want it to have been purposeful. I want to find out that someone was after him and that if they didn't get him that night, it would've been the next day."

Toni quietly asked, "Why?"

"Because then I couldn't have prevented it. I couldn't have stopped it by keeping him in the car a minute longer, keeping him happy, having him at the party with me instead of standing in the middle of the road."

Toni reached out and grabbed me by the shoulders. "It's not your fault, Morgan. It never was. You have to accept that. You want this so badly that you're pushing these crazy theories. You're going to go too far and hurt Evan. You're going to push him away and lose any chance at moving on. And, honestly, I think he's good for you. Better than Flynn ever was."

She was right. I knew she was right. And I was wrong to break in here. Evan had been nothing but straightforward with me—showing me the photograph with the warning on the back, bringing me to talk to that cop at the station, telling me the truth about his family. And I repaid him with betrayal. I felt sick.

"We have to get out of here," I said.

Toni's face lit up in agreement and then just as quickly shut down as we heard a thump in the hallway behind us.

I froze. Toni's widened eyes looked to me for instruction. I knew I should burst into action—move, run, something. But my feet were like lead, and my heart had stopped beating. Next came a scrape, the sound of a shoe sliding forward on the floor.

Someone was there, standing in the hall, equally frozen, listening for *us*.

I pointed at the window and motioned for Toni to get out first. If anyone went down for this, it had to be me. It had been my dumb idea. Toni stealthily slipped out without a noise. I shimmied out next, a bit clumsier. My shoe stuck on the window ledge, and my drop to the ground was anything but ninja-like. I got up, brushing mulch off my jeans. Toni was already down the grassy slope, halfway to the car. I started to run, casting one last glance over my shoulder.

A shadow stood in the window. Watching. I didn't stop. I kept on running, so hard my lungs ached, feeling the person's eyes on my back the whole way.

CHAPTER 22

Late Monday afternoon, Toni and I sat on the floor of my room, flipping through magazines. But all she wanted to talk about was our little adventure. As frightened as she'd been before the crime, she seemed proud of it afterward. She regaled me with the story again and again as if I hadn't been there myself.

"You should've seen your face when we heard a sound in the house," she said. "You were all . . ." She contorted her face into a grotesque expression of shock, and then doubled over laughing.

"It's not funny," I said, closing my magazine. "Someone saw us."

She shrugged. "We didn't get caught. You saw a shadow that could have been anything. If someone really saw us and recognized us, we wouldn't be in your room right now. We'd be at the police station."

Unless it had been Evan who saw us. He wouldn't turn me in. But it would be terrible just the same. I almost wished—if someone *had* to see—that it had been one of his parents. I'd rather have to apologize to them than face the shame of know-ing it was Evan watching me run from his house. I looked at my phone on the floor beside me. No blinking light. No new calls or messages.

"Hey," Toni said, "a watched phone never buzzes. Why don't you just call him?"

I flopped backward and stretched out on the floor, my eyes on the ceiling. "Because I did something horrible. I went tem-porarily insane. I don't even know what to say to him."

I'd felt nauseated all day, waiting for the phone or the door-bell to ring. I didn't want to call him because I didn't want to act like I'd done nothing. If someone had seen us, that would only make it worse. Deepen the lie.

"Are you going to stay for dinner?" I asked, changing the topic. "My mom is coming home at a good time tonight. She can make us some macaroni and cheese. Extra-orange, the way you like it."

"No, thanks. I have *secret* plans tonight." She wagged her eyebrows. Those plans involved Reece, I was sure. "You want to come along?" she asked.

The last thing I wanted was to be the third wheel at their love-apalooza. "Nah. I've had my fill of adventure for the week, and it's only Monday."

"Your loss," she teased.

"Yeah, yeah," I muttered.

She scrambled to her feet and grabbed her backpack. "I'm

going to head home and make an appearance, deal with questions about why I'm always out, break up an argument between Mom and Dad or Dad and Cooper, listen to some screaming, then go back out again."

"Sounds like a solid plan." I matched her sarcasm and went along with it because I knew that's what she liked. But my heart constricted. No matter how bad things got with my parents, my house was like a relaxing spa compared to hers.

Before she made it out the door, I called out to her, "Toni?"

She stopped and turned, her bag swinging in the air. "Yeah?"

"I love you, bestie."

Her mouth tightened, and for a moment I wondered if she was going to cry. Then she smiled. "Back at ya, babe."

I felt guilty for betraying Evan, but that didn't change how I felt about the things in Flynn's diary or my determination to get to the bottom of it. I scrolled through my cell until I found Cooper, then dialed him.

"*You* drive her," he answered.

"Um, what?" I said.

"My little sister wants a ride home. That's why you're calling, right?"

"No," I said. "She left already. I'm calling for something else."

He paused. "Oh, sorry. What's that?"

"Toni said you did a lot of research on Stell. For your college essay."

"Yeah . . ."

"Would you be willing to give me a quick rundown?"

"Sure. It was pretty simple. Their most profitable product, a migraine medicine, was sending a small percentage of patients into cardiac arrest. The guy at the top knew this, but covered it up. The money rolling in was too good to stop production. If the story got out, the company's reputation would've been shattered. So he considered that small percentage of dead customers collateral damage while he quietly worked on a fix for future batches."

"So what happened?" I asked.

"A whistleblower called the FDA. Named 'Employee X' in the legal proceedings, for protection. He or she blew the lid off the whole thing and the company went down. The CEO was going to be criminally charged before he offed himself."

"And that's it?"

"That's it."

It was the same story Evan had told me. No new information. I didn't know what angle Flynn had been working. The whole mess seemed to have been closed five years ago. I hung up with Cooper, and my mom called me down to eat.

Dinner with my parents was like a business meeting. We made small talk. They spoke about a local political race. I shared my thoughts on the history quiz I'd taken that day. I didn't ask them about the note, and they didn't act like someone had been sending them threats. On the surface, everything seemed happy and normal. And, to be honest, the calm made me feel temporarily better. Even if it was fake.

After dinner I went up to my room to do all the homework I should've done earlier with Toni. I left my reading till last and brought the assigned book into bed. Around ten, my eyes started to close. The book dropped to my chest.

My phone buzzed.

I shot up like a firecracker had gone off in my room. I grabbed at the phone clumsily, knocking it off my desk, then sank to the floor to get it. It was a text from Evan. My stomach clenched.

can you come outside now? in car one house down.

I opened my bedroom door. Blue light and soft voices came from my parents' room. They were watching TV, still awake. I'd have to sneak past them.

I typed back: be right there.

I pulled my hot mess of bed-head hair into a quick ponytail and threw a sweatshirt on over my tank top. My fleece pajama pants were red with white hearts—mildly embarrassing, but I didn't want to waste time changing. I snuck downstairs, carrying shoes in my hand, and slipped out the front door.

The night was mild and hummed with buzzing insects, the first sign that the long, quiet winter was coming to an end. Evan's car was parked in front of my neighbor's house. The interior light was off, and I couldn't see him inside. I thought I'd get in like I had the other night, but as I approached, he got out and stood up, closing the door behind him.

My nerves were on high alert, but I told my guilty conscience to chill. This little visit probably had nothing to do with what I had done. He'd found a clue. Or he just wanted to see me.

I stepped closer. His face showed no emotion, his mouth pressed into a thin line. He gave me a long look. The silence stretched between us like a rubber band about to snap.

"Hey . . . what's up?" I asked in a small voice.

He cleared his throat. "I have to talk to you, and I couldn't do it over the phone. I had to see you. See your face."

My hopes withered like a dying flower. He knew. He *knew.* "What about?"

"I forgot my glove," he said, his voice flat.

"What?" My mind spun in circles. He hadn't left a glove here. What was he talking about? But then I realized . . . he didn't mean here. He'd left it at his house on Sunday, when he needed it for his game.

"I came back just for a minute," he said sadly. "Figured I'd run in, grab my glove from my room, and run back out."

It was him. He was the shadow that watched me run away. And he obviously hadn't told his parents or turned me in. I braced myself for the words I knew would come next. The angry tone. I closed my eyes against it, but it never came.

When I reopened my eyes, he stood in the same spot. Not close-fisted and furious, but confused and hurt. The pain in his eyes was so sharp, I could barely take it.

"What were you doing?" he asked.

"I just . . . ," I stammered. "I wanted to see if I could find any clues."

Unreadable emotions flashed across his face, and he turned away from me. Tears sprang to my eyes. I had to explain. I had to make him understand.

I took a step forward, closing the distance between us. "In the car Saturday night, you seemed focused on Flynn's motives. How Flynn was out to get you guys. I thought you couldn't distance yourself enough to look at your own family. To see if there was anything *they* were hiding. Please. I don't want you to be mad at me."

Evan whipped back around. "Do you want to know what's sad about this whole thing? I'm not mad. I'm jealous."

I repeated, "Jealous?"

"Flynn lied to you about everything, and you assume he had the best intentions. Meanwhile I'm by your side, researching this even though it may hurt my own family. I keep no secrets from you, and you don't trust me."

"I *do* trust you," I said futilely.

"You have a funny way of showing it," he snapped back.

He was right. And if the roles were reversed, I wouldn't forgive him. I had to make this right.

I reached out for him with clammy hands.

"Morgan!" My mother's yell pierced the air. I looked and saw her standing in our front doorway, calling into the night. "Morgan!" she screamed, panic edging her voice.

Wonderful. I was in trouble with Evan for breaking in and in trouble with my parents for breaking out.

"I'm here!" I called back.

Mom came running down the front walk. Evan stiffened beside me and took a step back toward his car in the darkness.

"Morgan," she said with relief as she reached me. She grabbed my arms, like she was making sure I was real and not some illusion. I looked down and saw her bare feet on the sidewalk, and it finally sank in that something was going on. "Are you all right?" she cried.

"Yeah, Mom. I'm fine. What's going on?"

"It's Toni," she said breathlessly. "She's in the hospital."

CHAPTER 23
CHAPTER 23
CHAPTER 23
CHAPTER 23
CHAPTER 23

My stomach ached. My throat felt like it was filled with sand. I hadn't eaten in fourteen hours, but I still couldn't force anything down.

"Are you going to keep staring at that granola bar or are you going to eat it?" Cooper asked.

We'd been camped out in the hospital waiting room all night, watching other distraught families come and go. There was a boy with pneumonia, a girl with appendicitis, a man who'd had a heart attack. And us. Waiting helplessly for the teen with massive internal injuries, going through multiple surgeries all night long. We refused to go home. Refused to sleep. Refused to eat.

"You can have it." I passed the snack to Cooper. My dad had bought it from a vending machine and put it in my hand when I refused to go to the cafeteria with them.

I looked at Toni's parents. They were by themselves in the corner of the room, hugging and crying. I wanted to say something, but why bother? Words wouldn't help them right now.

Toni had been found by a trucker, lying in the middle of Crescent Road, bleeding. It made no sense to me. No one lived on Crescent Road. It was a dark and kind of deserted street on the edge of town with only a couple of industrial businesses. There was no reason for her to be there, never mind alone.

It was a hit-and-run.

Toni's "secret plans" hadn't been with Reece, as I'd assumed. And what made my heart feel like a lump of lead in my chest was that she'd asked me to go with her. If we'd been together, she might not be fighting for her life right now.

"Morgan? Can we speak to you, please?" My mom peeked her head in the doorway of the waiting room.

I stood, my body aching from being curled up in the same uncomfortable chair for hours. My parents had offered some polite words of hope to the Klanes, but other than that they'd been darting around like quiet hummingbirds. Keeping themselves busy. Getting people coffee. Making phone calls.

I hobbled into the hallway.

"We want to talk to you," Mom said.

I sighed. "I told you guys *and* the police—I don't know what she was doing there. I don't know where she was headed."

"Not about that," Dad said. "We want to know who you were with outside. Your mother said there was a car and a boy in the dark."

Oh. That. When Mom dropped the bomb about Toni being in the hospital, I ran to the house with barely a wave to Evan.

It wasn't exactly the time to do introductions. "Just a friend," I said.

"From school?" Mom asked.

"He goes to Littlefield High."

Dad frowned. "He's not just a friend if you're sneaking out to see him at night."

"Dad, please—"

He interrupted, "If you're going to continue to see this boy, he'd better have the manners to come in the house and introduce himself properly."

I couldn't tell them the true reason I was hiding Evan. I needed to get to the bottom of everything before I could parade him in front of my parents. But I had to tell them something now.

"He's afraid to meet you," I said. The lie came easily.

Dad narrowed his eyes. "Why?"

"His father worked for Stell. He feels awkward." Mom and Dad shared a quick look. "I told him you guys would never judge him for who his father is—"

"Who's his father?" Dad cut in.

"Darren Murphy."

Dad's eyes flared. "You can't see him anymore."

My mouth dropped open. "Wow. Real nice, Dad. I told Evan you guys wouldn't make a quick judgment, but here you are proving me wrong. And his father didn't even do anything, by the way. It was his uncle who screwed the company over."

Mom kept shaking her head, like an animatronic figure. "We're not going to discuss this," she said. "It's off the table."

"I'll see him anyway," I shot back. My bravado shocked me, but they were being so unfair. Acting like hypocrites.

I could see Dad's cheeks visibly flushing. "You're not going to sneak around like—"

I snapped, "Like you? All you and Mom are doing is sneaking around and keeping things from me. I know about the threats you've been getting."

Mom gasped. "How do you know about them?"

Them. So the note I saw wasn't even the only one.

The sound of footsteps made me turn. A doctor was purposefully marching this way. His face was unreadable. But as he turned into the waiting room, my parents and I dropped our fight to follow him.

Toni's parents jumped up from their seats, and Cooper ran over. "Is there news?" he asked.

The man spoke gravely. "I'm Dr. Chara. Toni pulled through her surgery."

If Mr. Klane hadn't had one arm around her, Toni's mom would've collapsed to the ground. "Oh, thank God," she said, hands clasped together.

"We're not out of the woods, though," the doctor continued. "Her brain swelling is significant. She's been put into a medically induced coma to help her body heal."

"For how long?" Mr. Klane asked, his face drawn tight.

"Until we can get the swelling down. You can see her now, if you'd like," the doctor continued. "One at a time, please."

Toni's mother went in first. I knew I'd have to wait until after both her father and Cooper had seen her as well.

Our argument temporarily forgotten, my mom whispered, "We're heading home, honey. You should come with us. Get some sleep."

I shook my head. "I need to see her."

Worry lines formed on Mom's forehead. "I don't know if that's a good idea."

My eyes pleaded with her. "I'm not leaving. I need to see her. I'll get a ride from someone else and meet you at home."

Mom nodded solemnly. "Don't stay too long. Her family probably wants to be alone."

My parents left, and I checked my phone. I had multiple texts from Evan. Even though he was mad at me, he was still clearly worried. I sent him a quick update. Then I called Reece again. He had skipped school and was pacing his house like a trapped animal. But he hadn't wanted to come to the hospital unless Toni's parents said it was okay. And things had been so touch and go over the last few hours, their daughter's boyfriend of the past few weeks wasn't really their top priority. I thought it was nice of him to give them their space, even though he was going out of his mind.

Cooper returned to the waiting room, wiping tears from his face with the palm of his hand. "Your turn," he said. "Nurse says five minutes only."

I shuffled to Toni's room, then paused outside the door. My nervous fingers held on to the doorjamb. As soon as I crossed the threshold and saw her, it would be real. I forced myself to move forward.

The hospital gown swallowed her tiny frame. Lying in the bed, her face pale, her blond hair fanned out across the pillow like an angel's halo, Toni looked like a child. A small, helpless, defenseless thing. I would do anything to protect her.

I lowered myself onto the chair beside her bed and willed my eyes to stay dry. I wanted to be strong for her. If she could hear me, I didn't want her to be scared.

"Hey, Toni. It's Morgan." I tried to sound happy, enthusiastic. It took all my effort to push down the panic, sadness, and anger that threatened to burst from me.

I ignored the alienlike tubes and IVs threading in and out of her body, the machines beeping in the background, and laced my fingers through hers. They were warm, but felt lifeless. It was unnatural to see her so still, her face so motionless. She was always talking, laughing, making animated expressions.

Memories like photographs flashed behind my eyes. Riding our bikes together, playing with dolls, dressing up in crazy costumes and putting on stupid plays in my room. We'd gone through everything together—school, first crushes, first heart-breaks. We told each other all our secrets.

She was more than my best friend. She was family. She was a part of me.

If I lost her . . .

I couldn't even let my mind go there.

My fist slammed down on the arm of the chair. I squeezed my eyes shut and took a deep breath, trying to calm down.

Then I looked again—at Toni's face, the blossomed bruise on her cheek, the gauze wrapped around her head. On closer inspection, I could see that her beautiful blond hair was long on only one side now. The other side had been shaved for surgery.

I bent over, gently kissed her forehead, and whispered, "I'm going to find out what happened. I promise."

I left the room, feeling as if my heart had split in two. I'd left half of it behind in that hospital bed. I would do anything to make it whole again.

Cooper hovered at the nurse's station, firing questions at a woman. She had just come in and was clipping her name badge on. I recognized her as the first nurse we'd talked to when we came in . . . how long had it been . . . sixteen hours ago? I had lost track of time. But she had gone home, slept, and was now back for her next shift.

"Was she conscious when she came in?" Cooper asked.

The nurse gave a slow shake of her head. "Barely."

Cooper pressed his fists onto the counter. "Did she say any-thing? Anything at all?"

"Just something about her mother. I assumed she wanted me to call your mom."

Cooper frowned. "Did she say that? 'Call my mother'?"

The nurse thought for a moment. "No. She just got out the word *mother*, then slipped away."

"Did—"

"Listen," she broke in. "I'm very sorry about your sister. But I need to go do my job and keep her alive right now. I don't know anything else about the accident."

She grabbed a file folder and walked away, but Cooper didn't move. His shoulders trembled. I figured he was crying, and I thought about going to him. But then he turned around, and I saw his face. There were no tears. Only pure, unfiltered rage.

I understood how he felt.

Cooper stormed back into the waiting room. And I figured it was time for me to let the Klanes be alone. I'd seen Toni and made my promise. Now it was time to follow through on it.

I left the hospital, the main doors hissing closed behind me. It was a beautiful, bright day, which felt so wrong. I wanted it to be dark and gloomy. The clouds should have been angry. The sky should have been crying.

I pulled my phone out of my pocket, thinking of who I should call to ask for a ride home when I stopped dead in my tracks. Evan was sitting on a bench outside the door. He gave a little wave when he saw me and slowly stood up.

He looked terrible. Gorgeous, still, but exhausted, like he'd been up all night.

"Any news?" he asked.

"They can't get her brain swelling to go down, so she's in a medically induced coma."

He crossed the distance between us in two swift steps and held my face in his hands. I thought he would kiss me, right there, but instead he pulled me to him.

"I'm so sorry," he said.

I pulled away. "No, *I'm* sorry. For what I did. For breaking into your house. I should've trusted you."

"No, I understand." He looked down at the ground. "I've been thinking. I shouldn't make you prove your trust to me. And Flynn . . . he was your boyfriend. You haven't known me as long. I have to keep reminding myself that we're in different time lines here."

Confused, I asked, "What do you mean?"

He shifted his weight from foot to foot. "I feel like I've known you much longer."

"Why?" I asked. He looked embarrassed, and I guessed, "The picture?"

He smiled sheepishly. "Despite the warning on the back, I used to stare at it, wondering who you were. Where you lived.

What your name was. Why I was supposed to stay away from you. I memorized every angle and curve to your face. I thought no one that beautiful could be dangerous."

I willed myself to look away, to break the eye contact that was making my heart stutter.

He brushed a lock of hair out of my face. "When you walked up to me at the party, it was like my best dream and my worst nightmare coming true at the same time."

"And now that you know I'm not out to get you?" I said.

He smiled, lighting up my heart again. A blush spread across his cheeks. "I understand that we're in different places," he said. "You spent these last few months grieving, and I spent them wondering about you. You were surprised by my existence, but I've been looking for you. Waiting for you. And now you're here and you're even better than the girl I made up in my head. I understand you need closure with Flynn. And I'll wait for you. Until you're ready."

I wasn't quite sure how to respond to this, and by his expression I could see that he was taking my hesitation as rejection. But it wasn't. Far from it.

Before my mind could stop me, I reached up and pulled his face to mine. I kissed him—eagerly, letting myself have everything I'd wanted over the last few weeks, not holding back. Right there in the parking lot, in front of I didn't care who. All I wanted was him.

He staggered a bit, shocked, but then his hands were on my

lower back, pulling me even tighter against him. His lips moving on mine felt like fire, and I was going to melt.

We broke apart to breathe. He bent over slightly, so our foreheads could touch. My eyes were on his mouth. My lips were aching for more.

He whispered, "Are you only kissing me because I look like him? Because you miss him and I'm the next best thing?"

My face felt hot, like the accusation was burning my skin. How could he even ask that? Couldn't he tell how much he affected me?

"No," I breathed. "I'm kissing you because you're you."

"Good. Because my heart's on the line right now."

"I'll be gentle," I said, and then went in for another kiss.

This one was less frantic and more tender. Perfect in every way. But after another minute, I started to feel guilty. Toni was inside the building, fighting for her life, and I was out here doing *this*. I pulled back and swallowed my emotions. This wasn't the time or place, no matter how badly I wanted it to continue.

Knowing what I needed, Evan wrapped his strong arms around me in a hug. I reveled in the feeling of his chest beneath my cheek, in his comfort.

"Were you up all night?" I asked.

"Yeah. I only came here about an hour ago, though."

I pulled back to look at him. "Where were you before? Home?"

"I went to Crescent Road, to see where it happened." He

swallowed hard. "I've been thinking. What if Toni found something?"

"I thought that, too," I said.

I'd been thinking it all night, and now that Evan did, too, I knew I wasn't crazy. What happened to Toni could not have been a coincidence.

My fists closed at my sides. Rage welled up inside of me, threatening to overflow. If someone did this to her on purpose . . . I could kill them.

"For your job with the paper, do you have a press pass or something?" Evan asked.

"I have an ID badge, yeah. Why?"

"I have to show you something."

"Where?"

"On Crescent Road."

CHAPTER 24

Evan pulled over to the side of the road and killed the engine.

"Why do I need this?" I asked, slipping the lanyard with my press ID attached over my head.

"Just so we don't look suspicious. Carry your camera. Take a few shots. If anyone shows up, you're taking pictures for the paper."

I got out of the car, camera held tightly in my hands, and took in the surroundings. Crescent was a quiet road on the outskirts of town, with an industrial look to it. A place called Bob's Tire Barn had boarded-up windows. Next to it was a gray building with a sign advertising M. G. Trucking, and beside that was Power Rentals, which—from the looks of it—rented bulldozers and other big machines. And that was it. No houses. No obvious reason why Toni would have been here. None of the businesses were even open at night. The street would have been totally deserted.

I focused on the empty road and snapped a photo.

Evan walked over and motioned to the right. "It's a dead end that way. So this is all there is."

"Maybe she was meeting someone," I said. "And they chose this road specifically because it was deserted."

"But who?" Evan asked.

"I have no idea. She joked about having secret plans, but invited me to come along." I choked on the last few words. "She was being a little silly so I thought she meant she was doing something with Reece. Why would she come here alone?"

"Maybe she didn't," Evan said darkly.

"Why would you say that?"

He walked to the center of the road and pointed. "This is where they found her."

There was a small stain on the asphalt.

"What do you see?" Evan asked.

I looked through the camera's lens, zooming in and back out. It was where Toni's blood had been. Where her life had leaked onto the road as she lay alone. I closed my eyes and took a shaky breath. I only hoped that she'd gone unconscious right after she was hit. I didn't want to think about her screaming in pain or feeling scared, calling out for help.

I opened my eyes and answered, "Toni's blood."

"What else?"

I took a cursory look around. "Nothing."

"I came here earlier. This is exactly what it looked like then.

When the police were still here." He paused as if that meant something.

"I'm not following," I said.

He pointed to the ground. "Shouldn't there be something here? Glass, maybe? Bits of plastic? Skid marks on the pavement?"

I let my eyes trail along the ground. He was right. There was literally nothing else around to indicate an accident. Only a small stain where her body had been. The scene was so . . . clean.

"Maybe it's all been cleaned up," I said.

Evan shook his head. "Last night, when we heard about what happened, you went to the hospital. I came straight here. I was here when the police were inspecting the scene. There should have been skid marks for them to measure. Tire tracks to photograph. Glass or plastic to sweep. There was nothing."

I racked my brain for an answer. "Do you think the person who hit her cleaned up before they took off?" No, that didn't make any sense. It was a hit-and-run, not a hit-and-stick-around-for-a-while-then-run. They wouldn't take the chance of being seen.

"You can't clean skid marks," Evan said. "There's some evidence you can't get rid of."

He already had a theory, I realized. "What are you thinking?"

"Would Toni really be walking down the middle of the road at night in the dark?"

"No way," I said, certain of it.

He nodded in agreement, then took a deep breath. "I don't think this is the crime scene. I think someone placed her body here to make it *look* like a hit-and-run."

Fear washed over me, freezing and numb, like slipping under ice. "They thought a hit-and-run wouldn't be as closely investigated."

Or maybe they *knew* it wouldn't be.

Because they'd done it before.

CHAPTER 25
CHAPTER 25
CHAPTER 25
CHAPTER 25

CHAPTER 25

Officer Reck's desk was just as dirty as it had been the first time Evan and I visited the station, but the cop himself looked more tired. Our little town didn't have many officers. He'd probably worked more hours than usual at the crime scene last night.

Reck listened attentively to Evan and me as we explained our theory, then sat stoically for a long moment, scratching at his goatee.

"What do you think?" Evan said, leaning forward in his chair.

"If your friend wasn't planning to be on Crescent Road, do you know where she *was* headed?" he asked.

"No," I answered. "She didn't tell anyone. But she had no reason to be there."

He looked down at the file. "Her injuries are comparable to being hit by a car."

Evan piped up. "But there's no evidence of an accident where her body was found. No broken glass. No tire marks. No blood splatter. Just the small puddle where her body lay."

"Her injuries were mostly internal, though," Reck said. "And as for the tire marks, the person probably didn't slam on the brakes because he or she never even saw her. The road has no streetlights. There's never anyone on it at night."

It wasn't unreasonable. Everything he said made sense, but I still wasn't convinced. A line from Flynn's diary repeated in my head.

Cops on the take.

I was done here. I stood, and Evan looked up quizzically. "That makes a lot of sense. Sorry to waste your time, Officer," I said.

Evan followed me outside, trotting to catch up. "Why didn't you want to push him harder? We could've tried to make him see our side."

I wanted to bring up the line from Flynn's journal. Evan had read it, too. But I'd already put him through enough by distrusting his family and breaking into his house.

"I just . . . I want to go." I turned to get into the car.

He put a hand on my wrist. "Hold up. What is it? You can tell me."

I gazed down at the pavement. "I know he's a family friend, but I don't trust him."

"You think he's covering something up?" Evan's voice wasn't defensive, just curious.

"You saw that line in Flynn's notebook. He could be dirty. Or maybe he's just lazy and doesn't want to deal with complications. He wants an easy case. I don't know. I only know he's not going to help me."

"Us," Evan corrected. He tilted my chin up until our eyes met. "I promised, remember? We will get to the bottom of this. Together."

He brushed his lips against mine, tentatively, as if waiting for me to tell him to stop. But I wouldn't. I couldn't. I lost myself in the feeling, lengthening the kiss and opening my mouth, morphing the moment from tentative to hot. I leaned back against the car. The length of his body pressing against mine felt so good, and I had a fluttery feeling in my heart that said *This is right.*

It nearly killed me to stop, but I had to. I pulled back and looked up at him. "I have to get back. I need to figure out a way to keep Toni protected."

He let out a slow breath and nodded, reluctantly stepping back. "I'm going to do some research of my own. Just promise me one thing."

He could've asked for almost anything at that point, and I'd have said yes. "What?"

He slid his hands gently down my arms. "Don't go anywhere

alone. Text me, and I'll come meet you. Wherever, whenever. I don't want you to . . ."

His voice trailed off, but I knew what he meant. He didn't want me to end up like Toni. Or Flynn.

I nodded. "Deal."

I paid for three coffees at the cashier in the hospital cafeteria and put them in one of those cardboard carriers. The smell reminded me of Flynn. He'd loved coffee, day or night—the caffeine didn't seem to affect him. I shook my head, refocusing on the task at hand, and searched the tables for the people I'd invited to meet me. I found Cooper sitting alone, his head resting on his arms.

"Is anyone with her right now?" I asked, placing the cups on the table.

Cooper slowly raised his head. His eyes were glassy and rimmed with red. "My mom is there," he croaked.

I handed him a coffee. He pulled the lid off, and steam wafted into the air, hovering like a ghost. I glanced around for my other invitee but he wasn't there yet. I didn't want to have to explain twice.

Cooper stared at the cup. "You know what her last words to me were?"

I flinched at the expression. "Last words" were said before someone died. Toni wasn't dead. But Cooper's face was an unreadable blur, a swirl of emotions simmering beneath the surface, and I didn't want to invite any of them to lash out. "What?" I asked.

"She said, 'Everything will work out. You'll see.' And now she's in a coma. She might *die.*"

It hurt me even more to watch his pain. "What was she re-assuring you about?"

He waved his hand as if it were unimportant now. "I got into Harvard."

Despite our situation, a smile broke through my dark cloud. This was a dream come true for Cooper. What he'd always wanted. "Congratulations, Coop! That's awesome!"

His face clouded. "I can't go."

"Toni will come out of this—"

"No," he said. "Even before this happened, I knew I couldn't go."

"Why?" I asked tentatively.

His eyes shot up to mine. "Why do you think? The money."

"But . . . financial aid?"

"It's not enough," he snapped.

I didn't have an answer to that. A cliché to placate him. Though Toni had tried, obviously. Even when things were at their worst, she was the eternal optimist. Her family was a mess. Cooper's lifelong dream was so close he could almost touch it, yet it was still unattainable. But she could always scrape up some enthusiasm.

"It's a gift," I said. "She always makes us feel better."

Cooper's wet eyes returned to staring at his untouched coffee. "What am I going to do without her?"

"You won't need to find out," I said with determination. "You won't."

"Morgan?" A voice called over my shoulder.

The conversation was about to get even worse. "Have a seat," I said, handing Reece the third cup.

"No, thanks. I don't drink coffee."

I placed it in front of him anyway and pointed across the table. "Reece, this is Toni's brother, Cooper." I motioned to my eyes, a signal to Reece that he should take his stupid sunglasses off.

"Oh, okay. Hey." Reece took off the Aviators and sat down.

"Cooper," I said, "this is Toni's boyfriend, Reece."

Cooper's shoulders went rigid. I knew he was about to launch into his overprotective brother shtick.

"Be nice," I said quickly. "He's going to be your only chance to sleep."

They both looked at me and said, "What?"

I heaved a sigh. Time to tell. "Evan and I went down to Crescent Road."

"I don't know why she was there," Reece started, his voice filled with frustration. "It makes no sense."

"I agree," I said. "She wouldn't be hanging around that area alone. And she certainly wouldn't be walking down the middle of a dark road with no streetlights. But that's exactly how the police are explaining why there are no skid marks on the road. No signs of a car trying to swerve or stop."

Cooper's brow creased. "That's weird."

"Weirder still," I continued, "there's no sign of a car accident at all. No shards of glass. No piece of a bumper or a headlight. Nothing."

Reece straightened in his seat. "What does that mean?"

"It means her body was moved," Cooper said, catching on quickly.

Reece shook his head in disbelief. "Why would someone do that?"

"To cover up the real crime scene," I said. "I think this was intentional. It wasn't an accident. She was targeted, and the whole thing was made to look like a hit-and-run."

Cooper's hands had been lying flat on the table. Now they tightened into fists. "Whoever did this," he snarled, "is as good as dead."

I put a hand over one of his. I didn't need anyone to lose control yet. "First things first. We have to make sure this person doesn't come back and finish what they started. The police won't put a guard on her door because they're convinced she's not at risk. But she is. And that's where both of you come in."

Without hesitation, Reece stood up. "I'll take the first shift."

Cooper stared him down for a moment, then nodded.

Reece grabbed the cup. "Time for me to start liking coffee."

CHAPTER 26

I clocked a few hours of sleep, mostly because my parents made me. Our fight about Evan moved to the back burner since we were all focused on Toni. But that didn't stop them from being, well, good parents and making sure I ate and slept and all those normal human things. At least they agreed to let me skip another day of school.

I quickly showered and dressed, letting my wet hair hang in clumps down my shoulders, then headed back to the hospital. Toni looked the same, and my eyes avoided her body in the bed. I didn't want to break down. I had to stay strong.

Reece noticed me and rose wordlessly, leading me into the hallway. The bags under his eyes were shiny and purple, like he'd boxed a few rounds and lost.

"Did you bring me more of that coffee?" he asked.

I smirked. "Addicted already?"

"I'll drink whatever swill I can to stay awake for her."

There was a desperate edge to his voice, and I was glad I'd

offered him this job. Otherwise, he'd drive himself insane. At least this way, he felt like he was doing something.

"No more coffee," I said. "Cooper should be here any minute to take over. You have to go home and sleep so you can come back tonight."

He nodded. "No problem."

"Nothing happened overnight?"

"No, but that doesn't mean this person won't try some other time. I want someone with her every minute."

"There will be," I said. "And believe me. However protective you feel about Toni, multiply that by a thousand and that's how her brother feels."

That seemed to lighten his burden a bit. His shoulders relaxed, and he ran a hand through his greasy, unshowered hair.

I peered through the doorway. Without the machines and the bandages, you'd just think she was sleeping peacefully, not in a coma, not clinging to the space between life and death.

"You know what bothers me the most?" I said. "That she was out there alone. Without me. Without you."

Reece's voice hitched. "She was getting me a present."

I looked at him. "What?"

"My birthday's coming up, and she said she was getting me 'what I always wanted.' That's all I know. She wouldn't tell me what it was or where she was getting it. And then this happened."

He looked very close to breaking, his lips trembling, his eyes full of self-loathing. I recognized that look. My jaw tightened. "Don't. You. Dare."

He startled, taken aback by my tone. "What?"

I pointed at his chest. "Don't you dare blame this on your-self. You didn't cause this."

He cast his eyes down. "Yeah, sure."

I knew my words wouldn't convince him, only time would. But Reece didn't deserve to feel the guilt I'd felt about Flynn's death.

We couldn't know where Toni had gone or what she was do-ing that got her into trouble, but it was not Reece's fault. Toni was completely selfless for those she loved. She'd go anywhere, do anything to make them happy. She even broke into Evan's house with me because I'd asked her to.

A tingle in the back of my mind made me stop, like my sub-conscious had already clicked things together and was just waiting for me to catch up.

"Hey," Cooper said, rushing up to us. "Any change?"

"No," Reece said. "No visitors either."

"Go home and get some sleep," Cooper said. "I'll take the next twelve hours."

Then Cooper noticed me, standing stiff. I hadn't even greeted him. I'd been silently planning my next move.

"What's up with you?" Cooper asked.

"Hold on." I walked a few steps away and called Evan's cell. It rang a few times and went to voice mail.

I returned to Cooper and Reece, who were looking at me strangely. "Hey, Reece," I said. "Do you think you could stay awake for one more hour?" I'd promised Evan I wouldn't go anywhere alone.

Reece shrugged. "Yeah, why?"

"I need you to help me. I think I know where Toni went."

Twenty minutes later, I rolled my car to a stop by the side of the road.

Reece raised his eyebrows. "What are we doing *here*?"

I glanced out the window. "I think this was going to be your birthday present."

Reece got out of the car and leaned against it, his arms crossed. I followed and stood beside him. We gazed up at the "King Mother" of all unoccupied houses behind its black iron gate. The huge house that Reece wanted to throw a party in someday, after he figured out some logistics.

"When Toni first got to the hospital," I said, "she tried to tell the nurses something, but they could only make out the word *mother*. They assumed Toni was asking them to call her mother. But maybe—"

Reece picked up where I left off. "She was trying to tell us what happened." He grimaced. "She said she was arranging my birthday present and it was something I'd always wanted. So, yeah, that part makes sense. Maybe she was going to throw me a party here, but she wanted to break in first and check things out."

He thought for a moment, then shook his head. "Nah. I can't picture her breaking and entering. That's just . . . not her."

I slowly raised my hand. "That would be my bad influence. I . . . uh . . . made her break into Evan's house with me. Long story. But it was easy, and she seemed pretty excited about it the next day. And that's when she went out for this secret mission of hers." I stopped and took a breath. "It's my fault."

Reece shook his head. "We both planted the idea, but you were right. It's not our fault. Whoever hurt her . . . it's their fault."

I returned my attention to the house. "So what do we do now?"

With fresh determination on his face, Reece pushed himself off the car and looked at me. "We go in and see what she found."

We approached the gate, and I grabbed onto the bars. The elegant mansion—a rich cream color with blood red shutters, three stories high—sat on top of the hill. A driveway sloped gently down a grassy hill until it reached the black iron gate—very similar to the layout of Evan's property. But the spaces between the bars weren't as narrow. Tiny Toni could slip through, but Reece and I couldn't.

"We'll have to climb it," Reece said.

Before I knew what was happening, his hands were around my waist and he was effortlessly lifting me up. "Grab the bar at the top," he said through clenched teeth. "Then swing yourself over."

I did as he instructed as quickly as possible before fear or vertigo could make me freeze. But I let go too early and dropped hard to the grass on the other side.

"You okay?" Reece asked.

I nodded from the ground, my tailbone aching. I never would have made it over without the boost from Reece. I wondered how he was going to do this. But I forgot—he was an athlete. He jumped up several feet, grabbed the iron bars, and pulled himself over without so much as a grunt. He dropped to the ground quietly like a cat.

If he and Toni ever had kids, they would be 100 percent pure ninjas.

I was still on the grass, propped up on my elbows. He held a hand out and pulled me to standing. I brushed myself off and limp-followed him up the hill as he took control and charged ahead. After all, I'd only broken into *one* house. *He* was the master.

We followed the curve of a sunroom—shades drawn like all the other windows—to the back of the house. Reece was marching from window to window, squinting in each one.

"They're all locked," he said.

I groaned in disappointment. "What now?"

"There's a way," he said. "There's always a way."

I followed behind, having to take two steps for every one of Reece's giant strides.

"People never forget to lock their front door," he said. "They use a dead bolt and everything. But they don't realize that's the least likely way for an intruder to get in."

"What's the most likely?"

"Unlocked windows. Unsecured sliding glass doors." He stopped walking and gazed at something on the ground. "And basement bulkheads."

He yanked on the handle and the door moved, then groaned as it opened outward. Reece looked over his shoulder and smiled.

He went down the stairs first. At least we didn't need a flashlight. Enough outside light poured in, and there wasn't much to see. The basement was just a basement. It was empty, aside from a furnace and the usual equipment, and smelled musty.

I pointed at the wooden staircase that led to the first floor.

Reece nodded, then maneuvered himself in front of me so he'd go first. As we exited the stairwell onto the first floor, I had a shock. It wasn't empty. The living room was fully furnished, including a flat-screen hanging on the wall.

"I thought you said no one lived here," I whispered.

Reece's face looked equally confused. "My buddy said no one has lived here for years. And I even staked out the house a few times and never saw anyone."

"Then why is it furnished?"

"Maybe the previous owner left the furniture? Maybe someone still owns it but they live somewhere else?"

We turned into the kitchen next. The dining area had no
furniture, but pots and pans hung from the ceiling above an
island. A stool was pushed out from the counter as if someone
had gotten up in a hurry and didn't push it back in.

I stepped over to the island, then stopped short. I shot my
hand out, frantically grabbed Reece's arm, and pointed to a
mug still steaming on the counter. I let out a high-pitched, panicked noise. "Someone's here."

That's what Toni found out. She came here looking for a
way to throw a party for Reece and found that the house wasn't
unoccupied after all.

I slowly turned around. The person was probably still in the
house. He or she heard us coming in . . . and hid. Or went to get
a weapon. My mind whirred with the possibilities.

"What should we do?" I whispered. Part of me wanted to
run around the house screaming in anger, opening the doors,
wildly looking in every nook and cranny until I found the person and made them pay. But I could hear Toni's voice in the
back of my head pleading. *Don't be stupid. Don't end up like
me. Get out.*

"We're leaving," Reece whispered back. "We can bring the
cops back with us."

That was the smart move. Despite how much I wanted to

be stupid. I just couldn't. For my parents. For Toni. For Evan. I had to get out alive.

A floorboard creaked in the other room, near the entrance to the basement.

Reece took my hand and pulled me behind him, leading us in the opposite direction. If that person was waiting for us where we came in, we'd find another way to leave.

Reece opened a door, saw that it was only a pantry, and moved on. The next door opened into the three-car garage I saw on the way up the hill. We went down a couple of steps into the cavernous room, Reece practically shoving me ahead, but I stopped and gasped.

"What?" Reece hissed.

I was surrounded by air, precious oxygen, but I couldn't seem to get any of it into my lungs. I pointed to the car parked in the only occupied spot in the garage. It was a black SUV with tinted windows. The car I'd seen enough times now to know this was not a coincidence.

Reece, thinking I was only pointing out further evidence of someone living in the supposedly abandoned home, yanked on my hand. He pulled my paralyzed body out the garage's side door and down the driveway.

But not before I got a good look at the license plate.

CHAPTER 27

CHAPTER 27

CHAPTER 27

CHAPTER 27

CHAPTER 27

We climbed back over the fence and Reece stuffed me into the passenger side of my car, knowing I was in no condition to drive. He pulled away, spewing dirt and dust up from under the tires.

"We're going straight to the police," he said. "And we're not taking no for an answer. We're dragging someone back here."

My heartbeat thrummed, reverberating through my whole body. The black SUV—it connected Flynn's death and the attack on Toni. Whoever lived in that house was the person responsible. I was so close now. *Secrets always reveal themselves.*

Now that my brain was moderately working again, I pulled out my cell and dialed Cooper's number. He answered from Toni's hospital room. "Yeah?"

"I know where she went," I said breathlessly. "It's a long story, but there's a house we thought was empty. And it's not. Can you find out whose name is on the deed without leaving Toni's side?"

"I can call a friend at work, yeah," he said. "Give me the address."

I did, and he promised to call back.

My right leg bounced up and down in the seat as Reece careened around curves and blew a light. As we pulled into the parking lot of the police station, my phone chirped. I answered, "Coop?"

"The house belongs to some corporation in the Caribbean," he said. "DD Exports. I can't find any information on them."

A company? "Why would they want a house in River's End?" I asked.

"I don't know. As a rental property or investment maybe?"

Was some shady company running an illegal operation out of that house? And Toni saw something worth killing her over? I couldn't wrap my head around it.

"Okay. We're headed to the police station. I'll fill you in as soon as I can. Don't leave her."

I marched into the station with Reece at my heels. But before I could approach the reception window and beg for help, the door opened and Officer Reck stood towering before me.

"Back again, Miss Tulley?" he asked.

The start of a headache stirred in my temple. I'd never told him my last name, had I?

Beside me, Reece let out a sigh of relief, assuming the cop and I were on good terms. "Officer," he said, "we need your help."

I tried to give Reece a look that said *No, not him,* but the details of our morning poured out of his mouth.

Officer Reck laid a giant hand on Reece's shoulder. "Okay, okay, calm down. Where's this house?"

He wrote the address on a little pad of paper as Reece recited it. Then he handed the paper to the woman at the dispatch desk. "Send a squad car or two to this address, please, and have them detain anyone on the premises."

He turned back to Reece and me. "Let's go to my desk."

We followed him to the now-familiar desk, littered with Styrofoam cups, tucked in the corner of the station. "Now, why are you so sure this was where your friend went the night she was hit by a car?" he asked, lowering himself onto his chair.

"She wasn't hit by a car," I said. "I told you that before and you didn't believe me."

"Did you find evidence of a crime at this house?"

"Well, no," I said. "But we didn't get a chance to look around much. We realized someone else was there and took off."

"How did you get into the house?"

I paled, starting to regret coming here.

Reece spoke up. "The front door was wide-open."

"And there's something else," I said. "The car that hit my ex-boyfriend—I saw it in the garage."

Reck scratched at his goatee casually. I almost expected him to yawn. "At that house?"

"Yes!" I felt like I was just spinning my wheels here.

Reck narrowed his eyes. "I thought you couldn't identify the car from the hit-and-run. I thought you didn't get a plate."

"I didn't. Well, not that night. But I've seen the car a couple of times since. One time it followed me."

"And it was the same license plate each time?"

"Well, no. I never saw the plate until today."

"So you can't actually confirm this is the same SUV." He gave a small shake of his head to let me know what he thought of me wasting his precious time. "Do you know how many black SUVs are in the area?"

"Can you just run the plate?" I snapped. I grabbed a Post-it from his desk and jotted down the memorized numbers.

I pushed it across his desk. "Please."

He looked at Reece, with an expression on his face that said, *Can you believe this emotional crazy girl?* He was probably hoping for some guy camaraderie, but instead Reece said, "Run it," in a tone that said, *If she's crazy, so am I.*

Reck let out a sigh so exaggerated, it was like we'd asked him to babysit quadruplets, not to—you know—do his *job*. He rummaged around in a drawer, finally pulling out a giant pair of eyeglasses. He slipped them on, and his fingers slowly punched in the numbers from the Post-it. Then he tilted his head back and forth, cracking his neck, while we waited for something to happen on the computer.

I saw a flicker of blue as the screen changed.

He clucked his tongue. "You must have memorized it wrong. Nothing's coming up. The screen's blank."

I sat motionless and tight-lipped, though inside I was burning.

The desk phone rang and he picked it up. "Yep." He paused as he listened to the voice on the other end. "Okay. I'll take care of it."

He hung up the phone and looked at us. "There's no one at the house now. A unit will stay on hand. If the person comes back, we'll detain them and see if they know anything about your friend."

Reece turned to me, his face twisted in frustration. I could tell he was expecting me to explode. To scream that this wasn't good enough.

Instead, I rose from my seat. "Thank you, Officer. You've been a big help. We'll leave it in your hands now."

I briskly walked away, trying to keep my face unreadable, until we got outside and Reece sidled up to me. "Morgan? What the hell just happened in there?"

"He's involved," I said.

Reece blinked quickly. "How do you know?"

"Because the SUV *did* come up on the screen. I saw words reflected in his glasses."

"Could you read them?"

"They were backward, so mostly no. But I clearly saw 'DD.'"

"It's a company car," Reece said. "DD Exports."

What was going on here?

I parked next to Reece's car in the hospital parking lot.

He clawed his fingers down his face. "I need to sleep. I can't even focus right now."

I gave him a reassuring pat on the shoulder. *I* was exhausted and I'd actually gotten a few hours. "Yeah, I know. That's why I just brought you back to your car. Go home. Sleep."

He rolled his head to the side and eyeballed me.

"What?" I said.

"Don't do anything stupid. Don't go back to that house. We'll figure this out, but our top priority has to be staying safe. Something's going on, and people who get too close to the answer end up . . ." He aimed a thumb at the hospital building behind him. "And Toni would murder me if anything happened to you while I was taking a nap."

I snorted. "Don't worry. Get some sleep. I'll be good."

He heaved a sigh and dragged himself out of my car and to his own.

I would be safe, but I wouldn't give up. I had to keep digging.

My phone buzzed from the pocket of my jeans. I hadn't heard from Evan all morning. It had to be him. I looked down and felt a twinge of anxiety. It was an anonymous text from a restricted number.

Meet me at The Falls in an hour. I can help you. I have information.

An eerie feeling swept over me, like the cool breath of a ghost, causing goose bumps to spring up on my arms. It was too easy. It had to be a trap.

But it wasn't a threat—like, *Meet me here or so-and-so dies, come alone.* It was worded like an offer.

I read the text over and over until finally coming to a decision. I couldn't let this opportunity go. The truth was so close now. But I wouldn't go alone.

I texted Evan.

are you around?

After a long minute, he wrote back.

not right now. y?

My fingers flew over the phone.

got a weird text. some1 wants me 2 meet them at the falls in 1 hr. i need 2 go. I need answers.

He responded quickly.

not without me. i'll meet u there. i'm 45 mins away.

Where is he? I thought. But before I could ask, another text came in.

in nh. bringing back answers for you like i promised. see u soon.

Evan had gone to *New Hampshire*? I stuck the phone back in my pocket and held my hands out in front of me. They were shaking. My nerves were on edge, and I felt like my heart was beating double time. The answers were so close now.

But a small voice whispered from the back of my mind.

I bet that's what Flynn thought, too.

I parked next to Evan's car. His was the only other one in the lot, so unless my mystery informer was hiking through the woods, he or she wasn't here yet. I took the path, tossing uneasy looks over my shoulder, until it opened up at the top of the waterfall. Evan stood, nervously shuffling his feet. When he saw me, he jogged over.

"You're here!" He pulled me into his arms, but let go too quickly. "Did you see anyone else?"

I shook my head.

"How's Toni?"

"No change. But Cooper and Reece are taking turns watching over her so she's never alone."

"Good," he said.

"And I think I know where she went that night. Reece had his eye on this giant abandoned house—he wanted to throw a party there and she went to check it out. But it wasn't abandoned after all. The car that killed Flynn was there. Everything's coming together." I was speaking too quickly, the words rushing out of my mouth like the water raging down the falls beside us. "What did you find in New Hampshire?"

He pulled a folded piece of paper out of his back pocket. "I think this explains everything."

A branch snapped from somewhere behind me. Evan stopped and looked over my shoulder. His face was a battleground of emotions—fear, grief, betrayal—but shock won out.

He let out a ragged breath and said, "You *are* alive."

CHAPTER 28

CHAPTER 28

CHAPTER 28

CHAPTER 28

CHAPTER 28

I spun around to face the person, but what I saw only confused me more. *Evan's dad?*

"Mr. Murphy?" I said, my voice sounding so small against the backdrop of the rushing water.

He was dressed casually, in jeans and a gray hooded sweat-shirt, and walked confidently toward us, hands in his pockets. He laughed, as if my recognizing him was some kind of joke. And that made everything click into place. I was looking at a dead man.

"You're not Evan's dad," I said.

A grin pulled at the corner of his mouth, confirming the truth. This was Doyle Murphy. The man who'd disgraced his company and his family and thrown himself off the top of the falls, in this very spot. Evan's uncle.

I shot Evan a look. "You knew about this?"

"Not until today," he said. "Not until this." He handed me the paper he'd been holding. I unfolded it, and the world spun.

It was James Bergeron's birth certificate. Flynn's birth certificate. And Doyle Murphy was his father. Flynn and Evan were first cousins, and their fathers were twins. I tried to swallow, but my throat was dry as dust.

Evan positioned himself in front of me, fists balled at his sides. "How can you be alive?"

Doyle kept his voice neutral. "They never found my body, Evan."

"The current took it away," Evan said. "Your blood was all over the rock."

Even though the impossible was staring him in the face, Evan couldn't seem to accept it. Or maybe he just needed to hear an explanation. I did, too.

Doyle gave his nephew a long, cool stare. "It's easy to get a bag of your own blood when you donate on a regular basis."

"You stole your own blood?" Evan asked in disbelief.

"It had to look legitimate. My DNA had to be on that rock. I spilled the blood, made the anonymous call that I saw a jumper at the falls, then took a private off-the-books flight to Grand Cayman."

The calm tone of his voice didn't match the tension in his shoulders, his stiff jaw, and his wild eyes. He wasn't as confident as he'd like us to believe. Underneath, he was a live wire.

"So why are you back now?" Evan asked.

"Now?" He gave a derisive laugh. "I've been back and forth

several times. I even watched one of your games. I just had to make sure your dad wouldn't be there. The two of us can't be in the same place at the same time."

Evan considered that for a moment. "Does my dad know you're alive?"

"He didn't at first," Doyle said. "I tried my best to protect him. And I actually never planned on coming back. But there I was, sitting on top of a pile of money in the Caribbean, warmed by the sun, surrounded by the most beautiful blue water you'd ever seen . . . and I might as well have been in prison. I got homesick."

He shook his head at the absurdity of it. "I wasn't a free man. Not if I couldn't come home now and then. Not if I couldn't see my brother. Watch my niece and nephew grow up. If I stayed away, you'd forget me. So I came and went—private charters, using your father's passport. I purchased a beautiful foreclosed home for a steal, under a shell corporation's name. And I stayed there when I came to visit. But then . . ." He paused for a breath. "Then things started to get complicated. Your father figured out what I'd done."

I stayed completely still, as if any movement would stop him from talking.

"What did he do?" Evan asked.

"He told me to stay away. He was nervous, scared that if the law found out I'd faked my death, they'd take him down with me. That was always his worry. Even growing up, Darren was always worried he'd catch the blame when I got into trouble. But he never did anything wrong. Not even at Stell. If he'd known about the deaths we caused, he'd have shut down production and reported it immediately. That's why we're a good team. We balance each other out. Darren does the right thing, and I do what needs to be done."

Evan had said he thought his dad was hiding something. That he'd go through periods of unexplained anxiety. Now we knew he got nervous when his brother was in town.

But why was Doyle telling us everything now? Had he decided to come back from the dead? Make things right?

"Dad wasn't the only one to find you," Evan said.

Doyle's face darkened, and I knew. This little speech wasn't about contrition. Fear spread through my body.

"No." He groaned and rubbed his cheeks. "The boy found me. He came right up to my house. I pretended to be Darren, of course, but he had all sorts of questions, and I knew he wasn't going to give up."

Evan's voice cracked, "He was your son."

"He was a mistake I made nearly two decades ago one night with a woman I didn't even know," Doyle spat. "That doesn't make someone family. I offered him money, but the poor kid"—he stopped to let out a callous snort—"he didn't want money. He wanted *me*."

Doyle shook his head at the thought. "It was sad, really. He thought I'd turn myself in, face the charges, give up my money.

That I'd go public and sacrifice everything to welcome some whore's kid."

"He was your blood!" Evan raged. He lashed out and grabbed Doyle's sweatshirt in his fists. *"My* blood!"

Doyle broke out of Evan's hold and shoved him back, sending a rock skittering over the edge of the falls. "You spoiled brat, can't you see that I protected you? If I went public with the news that I'd faked my death, your family would be dragged through the mud again. Your father might be charged with aiding and abetting a criminal. You could lose your house, money for your future, your dad."

"But James was my family and you killed him!" Evan roared.

Doyle held out his hands innocently, that cocky-calm look returning to his face. *"I* didn't kill him."

"Not yourself, no," I said, finally gaining the courage to speak up. "You got Officer Reck to do it for you."

His eyes flicked to mine in surprise. He looked almost impressed. "I told him to take care of the problem. How he got that done was his own choosing."

"And Toni?" I shot back.

He shrugged. "Your little blond friend saw too much."

"She saw you alive in your house," I guessed.

"And then she accidentally fell out a second-story window onto the driveway."

"You're a psychopath!" Evan yelled, and the water behind him seemed to rage even louder.

Doyle considered this. "You know they say that three to five percent of all CEOs are psychopaths?" He waved his hand dismissively. "I'm driven. That's the difference between your father and me. We'd never have made it as far as we did with his by-the-books thinking. I'm spontaneous. I'm the problem solver. I get things done."

He returned his attention to me. "And I just have one last problem to get rid of. I'm really sorry that it's come to this, Morgan, but . . ." A slow smile spread across his face. "It's also kind of . . . karmic."

Tension seeped into my muscles. "What did I ever do to you?"

"You don't know?" He threw his head back and looked up at the sky. "Oh, that's rich."

"What?" Evan said. He reached out behind him, blindly searching for my hand.

Doyle pointed from Evan to me. "Look at you two. The Montagues and Capulets." He sneered, "Noah Tulley, this girl's father, is the reason for our family's downfall. He ruined Stell. He destroyed the town."

I shook my head quickly, not understanding.

"Stupid girl," he snarled. "Your father is Employee X."

My head started throbbing. Dad was the whistleblower? Was that the secret my parents whispered about at night? The thing they didn't want me to know?

It was my father who'd set things in motion, and Flynn had

found out. I remembered the line in his notebook that read like algebra: $NT=X$.

I imagined the struggle my dad went through after he found out people were dying because of Stell. The choice that lay before him. Speak up and ruin everything. Or stay silent and be complicit in the deaths of innocents.

I'm sure it wasn't easy. Pride welled up inside of me.

I glared at Doyle. "You sent those notes to my parents. You tried to scare them."

"What notes?" he asked.

"My parents did nothing wrong," I insisted, anger edging my voice.

He took a lumbering step toward me, causing Evan to stiffen. "Your father should've waited. No one had to know. I was fixing things behind the scenes. The next batch of pills would have been better. The company would have survived. The town wouldn't be rotting. So many lives have been destroyed because of your father."

"No," I said. "Because of *you*. What my father did was brave. He did the right thing. He saved lives."

Evan put his body between me and his uncle. Evan was much younger and slightly bigger. All he had to do was stay away from the edge, wrestle Doyle to the ground, and I could call for help.

"You're not going to touch her," Evan said fiercely.

Disappointment dimmed his uncle's eyes. "You'd choose her over your family?"

"I choose her over *you.*"

Raw fury contorted Doyle's face and, quick as lightning, he struck out his fist and hit Evan straight in the jaw. Evan didn't even have time to react. He slumped to the ground, unconscious.

A small cry escaped from my mouth.

"Just a little trick I learned," Doyle said, glancing down at Evan's body. "Cranial nerve strike. Something they don't teach the boys in baseball camp."

The wind changed direction and spray misted my face. I blinked against the wetness, wiping at it with the back of my hand. Blood rushed loudly through my head, mixing with the roar of the falls.

Doyle's attention shifted back to me. I looked up at his hulking frame and my legs turned to jelly. My mind searched for strategies, for any way out. As if reading my thoughts, Doyle said icily, "You can run, but I'm faster. You can fight, but I'm stronger."

I put my hands up in front of me, as if that could ward him off. "There have been too many deaths. It'll look suspicious."

"There are only so many ways to make a death seem accidental, yes." He advanced on me as he spoke. And with each step, I took one backward, closer to the ledge, to the churning, foaming water below. "There are cars, of course, but one more of those would seem . . . suspicious, you're right. That's why you, my dear, are going to kill yourself here."

"No," I said, my voice quivering. "They'd never believe it."

He spoke in a monotone, like a news anchor explaining the nightly tragedy. "You got the idea when you took pictures for the paper last week. You've been so distraught over the death of your ex-boyfriend that you came here and . . . jumped. Officer Reck will tell everyone how obsessed you were. How you'd deluded yourself into thinking your boy toy was still alive. How depressed you were when you found out that he wasn't. No one will question your death." He smiled slowly. "They never questioned mine."

I looked over at Evan on the ground, hoping to see some sign of life, but he lay still. "Evan won't go along with your story."

"By the time he wakes up, I'll be gone. It's time to revisit some of my favorite secluded international beaches. This particular trip to River's End was more trouble than it was worth. If Darren wants to *stay* out of trouble, he'll find a way to keep his boy quiet. If he can't, I just won't return. And good luck to anyone who tries to find me."

He shrugged like it was no big deal. He was completely void of empathy. For his customers who'd died. For Flynn, Toni . . . or me.

The wind whipped up the back of my shirt as the falls roared behind me. I was at the edge. Nowhere else to go. I fell to my knees. The stupid girl in the horror movie, giving up, begging for her life. I put my hands up. "Please, Mr. Murphy. Please don't." Tears sprang to my eyes. Real tears.

But the giving up?

That part was an act.

Doyle reared up, ready to kick me over the side. I could see it, in my mind's eye. Me falling backward, gliding through the air, wind whipping my hair over my face, the water swallowing me whole.

But as his foot neared my torso, I grabbed it in midair. I twisted his leg with all of my strength and rolled myself to the side, pressing my body to the ground. He tried to right himself, find a new balance, but the momentum he'd built up to kick me propelled his own body over the side.

He fell through the air, not gracefully, but clawing, screaming, clinging to life—until a jagged rock silenced him, and the water pulled him under.

I scrambled over to Evan on my hands and knees and pulled his head onto my lap.

"Evan?" I said, rubbing his cheek hard. "Wake up, Evan."

His eyes fluttered open and for one last second they were Flynn's eyes. Gray and mysterious. Skeptical and untrusting. Then his lids closed slowly, like a drawn window shade, only to snap open again.

"Are you okay?" he managed to push out.

"Yeah," I breathed. "He's . . . gone."

I leaned over and covered his forehead, his nose, his eyes, his cheeks with kisses.

I wasn't drawn to Evan because of any similarities to Flynn. Other than their looks, they were complete opposites. I understood now why Flynn never let me in. But his secretive nature had made me feel insecure. Evan made me feel . . . *everything*. Beautiful. Wanted. Worthy. Deserving of someone like him. And I realized, in an intense full-bodied rush, like a first breath after being underwater, that I loved him. I was in love for the first time in my life.

I opened my mouth to tell him, but he spoke first.

"I love you, Morgan."

CHAPTER 29

Evan drove, one hand on the wheel, one hand holding mine.

I watched the town go by through the window. We passed the police station, with three media vans parked out front, and kept going toward our destination.

Several days had passed since Doyle Murphy went over the falls. This time, they found his body. We told the police everything Doyle had admitted at the falls. That, combined with some interesting bank deposit records, led to the arrest of Officer Reck. A media frenzy descended on the town. The story of the not-so-dead CEO was appearing on national nightly news programs. Word around town was that they were even writing a made-for-TV movie. River's End would be famous.

Evan and I had pulled together the information he'd gotten in New Hampshire with what we learned from his uncle, and now we knew the whole truth. Everything I'd wanted to know about Flynn.

James/Flynn was born to a single mother. Doyle was his biological father, but he paid his one-night stand off in one lump sum. James and his mother lived a happy life in small-town New Hampshire until she died from cancer and he ended up in foster care at seventeen. Lonely and unhappy, he researched his father's identity and learned that he, too, was dead. But Flynn came to River's End anyway, in search of other relatives, maybe some real family. Instead he found his father, alive.

Doyle Murphy faked his death to avoid paying for his crime and spent most of his time hiding in the Caribbean, coming home now and then posing as his brother to relax in his abandoned mansion on the hill. Everything was working fine. Until Flynn found him and his secret was threatened. Doyle tried to keep Flynn pacified with money and promises. But all Flynn really wanted was the one thing Doyle was unwilling to be—a father.

When Flynn started to suspect that he might be in danger, he wrote the note to me in his notebook and mailed the photo to Evan. He didn't want us to meet, to look into Flynn's background, to risk *our* lives. He just wanted us to forget him.

But we couldn't. And now I could grieve the real boy behind Flynn's mask: the boy who only wanted a place to belong.

My phone buzzed in my pocket and I pulled it out. A text from Mom.

Will you be home for dinner? I'm making lasagna.

I typed back:

sounds good. i'll be there.

A moment later, another text came through.

Evan is welcome to come, too.

I smiled. Now that I knew the secret my parents had been hiding, things had changed at home. We were working on our communication and being more open with one another.

I didn't blame my dad for his role as Employee X. It actually made me respect him more. Doing the right thing took a crazy amount of courage. What I *was* pissed about, though, was that they'd never told me, even after they'd started receiving threats. I know they only wanted to protect me, and that's something that will never go away, even when I'm their age, blah blah blah. But still.

And they were, of course, furious that I'd never let them in on the whole Evan/Flynn thing. So there was a lot of trust rebuilding going on. Starting with them trusting my judgment, letting me date Evan, and judging him on his own merits and not his family history.

My parents still didn't want people in town to know Dad was the whistleblower. Others might not be as understanding. Somehow, owning this secret together made us feel closer. Like we were a team.

Evan pulled the car into a parking spot. "I don't want to let you go," he said, squeezing my hand to prove his point.

We'd been inseparable since the day at the falls, seeing each other whenever we could and texting or talking on the phone when we were apart. I'd fallen hard and fast, Toni-style. The irony was not lost on me.

I leaned forward and pressed my lips against Evan's cheek, softly, then down his jawline, and finally on his mouth, which was eagerly awaiting mine. Then I pulled away and reached for the door handle.

He hesitated. "Are you sure you don't want me to go in with you?"

"I'm sure," I said. There was more than one thing I had to do. "See you soon."

I left the warmth of Evan's car for the sterility of the hospital. I nodded at the woman covering the nurse's desk—I knew them all by name now—and approached Toni's room. My footsteps echoed off the waxed floors as my pulse increased in speed. It didn't feel real. It had all turned so fast.

Her mother's cries carried out from the room. I peeked in the doorway. Toni's body was obscured by her mother's trembling, hunched-over frame. Her father stood one step away, a strong hand on his wife's shoulder.

"It'll be different now," Mrs. Klane said between choked sobs. "I promise. No more fighting. No more drinking. We're turning things around. Moving forward."

"It's about time," I heard Toni's voice say.

A huge smile broke out across my face. It was nice to see that she'd woken from her coma with her personality intact.

"Oh, good. Someone called you." Cooper appeared at my side, and we stepped away from her door.

"Yeah, your dad called," I said. "So she's okay?"

"The doctors thought it was safe to bring her out of the coma. The brain swelling's gone down. She still can't come home for a while. But they think she's going to be fine, yeah."

I let out a shaky breath. "Great."

Cooper's face turned serious. "I've been wanting to thank you. For making Reece and I keep watch. For getting the guy who did this."

"You know I'd do anything for her," I said.

"Yeah, I know. But . . . I owe you. If there's anything I can do to repay you, name it."

I hesitated, casting a nervous glance at Toni's doorway. The hall was empty. As much as I'd dreaded this conversation, I wanted to have it now, and quickly, before anyone interrupted us.

"Actually there is," I said. "You can stop sending threats to my parents."

"I don't . . . What do you mean?" he said, but his pale face and slack jaw were dead giveaways. Giving up, he asked, "How did you know it was me?"

The truth was I didn't know for sure until that moment. I'd

been thinking about it for days. Hardly anyone knew my father was Employee X. Doyle Murphy knew, but he'd confessed to everything at the falls and seemed legitimately confused when I brought up the notes. Flynn knew. But ghosts don't send notes. It had to have been someone who'd only recently found out. People don't start holding a grudge five years later. So I thought about Cooper and his Stell research. And the timing of my parents' weird behavior. And his parents' resentment. His anger over college and money.

I'd been hoping my instinct was wrong. Cooper was the last person I wanted it to be. But here it was. Disappointment dragged on my heart like an anchor.

"It doesn't matter how I know," I said. "I just want to know *why*. How could you do that to my parents?"

Red-faced with shame, he grabbed both my hands. "I'm so sorry, Morgan. I was just so angry. And it's not your dad's fault. I realize that. I'd let my parents' bitterness poison me. And Diana was mad that I couldn't be with her at school. And I . . ."

He let go of my hands and looked at the floor. "I needed someone to take it out on, I guess. I never would have really blackmailed them or anything." He gazed up at me, his eyes pleading. "Please don't tell Toni."

I didn't want to tell Toni. She'd been through enough. And she leaned on Cooper so much. I didn't want to be the one to tarnish him in her eyes. But was it enough to figure out who the anonymous person was and give my parents peace of mind? Did I also need him to be punished?

After a long moment, I said, "Fine. I won't say anything. But not for you. For her."

Mrs. Klane poked her head out of the doorway to Toni's room. "Oh, Morgan! She'd love to see you!"

I left Cooper alone with his regrets and crossed the threshold into Toni's room. I tugged the baseball hat I was wearing down tightly on my head. The room was overflowing with flowers, balloons, stuffed animals, and cards. The head of the bed was raised, and Toni sat with her hands clasped on her lap. The bandages were off, and she looked almost like herself. Especially when she smiled at me.

"Get in here," she ordered.

I swooped over and wrapped my arms around her as much as I could, remembering to be gentle. Then I pulled back and sat in the chair, wiping happy tears from my cheeks.

"How do you feel?" I asked.

"Like I fell from a second-story window," she joked.

Toni had already spoken to the police and corroborated what I'd heard at the falls. Doyle Murphy pushed her out the second-floor window of his hidey-mansion. Then he called Reck to clean up his mess and stage the scene on Crescent Road. She was lucky to be alive.

"I heard you killed the guy," she said in a low voice. "Evan's uncle."

I shrugged. "It was me or him, and it sure wasn't gonna be me."

She cracked a smile. "Look at you, being all badass-y."

"Look at you, being all alive-y," I said back.

She smiled, but her eyes got this faraway look, like they were reliving that dark moment. "I don't want to talk about me anymore," she said. "Tell me something about you. Something good. What have I missed?"

"I applied to the summer program."

Her face brightened. "You got off your lazy butt and submitted your portfolio? Go, you! Now please make my day and tell me you and Evan are an official thing."

I couldn't help smiling. "Yes, we are. You were right about him."

She cupped her hand over her ear. "Say that again. Just the last part."

I laughed. "You were right."

She leaned her head back on the pillow. "Man, that feels good. I might have the doctor give you instructions to tell me that every day."

"You are such a pain in my—"

She made a tent with her fingers and narrowed her eyes at me. "Have you given him the All-Access Pass to Morganland?"

I looked up at the ceiling and shook my head. "I think it's time for your pain pills."

She mock slammed a fist on the bed. "Come on! I need details!"

"You'll get nothing!" I stood up, pretending to go, but Toni reached out and grabbed my hand.

"You're so lucky I didn't die. You'd never find another best friend as awesome as me."

"Truth," I said, blinking back more tears.

She reached up and touched the shaved side of her head. "I am one hot mess."

"Just hot," I corrected.

She rolled her eyes. "Don't patronize me. My head is half-bald, Morgan."

"It's edgy! Five bucks says within a week, girls at school start copying you."

"Yeah, right," she snorted. "Who'd be insane enough to do that?"

I slowly reached up and took my baseball hat off. That morning, I'd cut my long black hair into a short bob and shaved the left side above the ear.

Toni's eyes nearly bulged out of her head. "No. You. Didn't."

"Reece did it, too," I said.

Her hand flew up to her mouth. "Are you serious?"

"Yep. He'll be here any minute. I'm so glad you're better.

He's been keeping the whole town awake with his incessant crying every night."

She burst into laughter and then winced and grabbed her side. "Ouch. Don't make me laugh."

I shrugged lightly, my shoulders barely lifting. "I'm your best friend. That's my job."

ACKNOWLEDGMENTS
ACKNOWLEDGMENTS
ACKNOWLEDGMENTS
ACKNOWLEDGMENTS

ACKNOWLEDGMENTS

High-fives and hugs to:

Everyone at Putnam, especially my editor Shauna Rossano.

My agent, Scott Miller.

Barbara and Dan Harrington, my biggest cheerleaders (also known as Mom and Dad).

My family and friends who make me laugh and fill my days with funny texts and e-mails, and who still come to my signings even though you're probably getting sick of them, but you know that I need you there. Love you guys.

Book lovers everywhere—readers, bloggers, librarians, teachers, booksellers. Thank you.

Mike and Ryan, the best things that ever happened to me, the two suns in my sky.